Mistakenly Matched

A NO MATCH FOR LOVE ROMANCE

LINDZEE ARMSTRONG

Snowflake
Press LLC

Also by Lindzee Armstrong

Visit lindzeearmstrong.com for a complete list!

SECOND CHANCES IN SAPPHIRE COVE SERIES

Promise to Stay

Dare to Fall

Refuse to Sink

Learn to Belong

NO MATCH FOR LOVE SERIES

Miss Match

Not Your Match

Mix 'N Match

Matched by Design

Match Me if You Can

Match Me by Christmas

ROYAL SECRETS SERIES

Taming the Prince

Dating the Prince

Winning Back the Princess

Marrying the King

CHASING TOMORROW SERIES

Chasing Someday

Tomorrow's Lullaby

"My heart is, and always will be, yours."

— JANE AUSTEN

Chapter One

How had she run out of ice cream? Kelsey hurried through the grocery store, avoiding eye contact with the few late-night shoppers as she made a B-Line for the freezer section. The harsh fluorescent lights glared down on her like a spotlight, screaming, *This woman is wearing her pajamas out in public!* When she'd left the house, she'd assured herself she could be in and out of the store in five minutes. Now that she was here, she was worried she would run into one of her co-workers from The Frosted Bride, or maybe a neighbor from her apartment complex. Jasmine, her best friend who lived just a few doors down, was a fashion designer and would die of horror if she saw Kelsey right now.

But Kelsey had just gotten back from Oklahoma a few hours ago and had a relaxing evening of reality TV planned to celebrate yet another successful wedding. Planning movie star Jase Larson's nuptials had been a major career boost for Kelsey, but she'd been a bundle of worry for the past eight months as her mind played an endless loop of things that could go wrong. At least Cassidy had been an extremely easy-going bride, and in the end, the wedding had turned out perfectly.

Pajamas or no, what Kelsey needed tonight was ice cream. *Eye in the Sky* wasn't the same without Dryer's slow churned. She scanned the

1

selections: mint chocolate chip, fudge tracks, cookies 'n cream. Her eyes stopped on rocky road, making her heart lurch.

That had always been Jadyn's favorite flavor.

Kelsey rubbed the spot behind her left ear with an index finger. She'd gotten the tattoo of a red balloon after the memorial service, determined to always keep a piece of Jadyn with her. Red balloons had sort of been their thing—a silly way to comfort each other when things got hard. It had started when they were only kids, and they'd kept up the tradition into adulthood. Sometimes it was actual balloons, but usually it was pajama pants with balloons, or red candy in the shape of a balloon, or a dozen other things. Funny that Kelsey hadn't been brave enough to get the tattoo until Jadyn was no longer around begging her to do it.

You hate rocky road, she reminded herself.

Kelsey was more sentimental than usual with the second anniversary of Jadyn's death approaching. But not sentimental enough to ruin her ice cream with almonds. Her eyes skipped over the rocky road and focused on the double fudge brownie.

"Jadyn?"

Oh no. Kelsey slowly turned around, wishing she could shoo the person away like an obnoxious fly. Of all the things she wanted to get into tonight, Jadyn's untimely demise was at the absolute bottom of her list.

In the twenty-two months since Jadyn's death, Kelsey had run into a few situations like this. Telling old acquaintances about her twin sister's passing never got easier. At least last time she'd managed not to cry. That was progress, and Kelsey prayed she'd be as successful now.

"It is you." Before Kelsey could get a good look at the man, he clasped her to him in an enthusiastic hug.

She let out a yelp of surprise, and the man pulled back.

"Sorry, didn't mean to startle you. It's me, Bryce. From band?"

Her stomach jumped like she'd just swallowed a packet of Pop Rocks, sending a *zing* of energy clear down to her toes. His brown hair was short on the sides and longer on top, replacing the shaggy mop from their high school days. A five o'clock shadow now covered his face, highlighting his strong jaw and straight nose. But she could see the Bryce of ten years ago hidden beneath. They hadn't talked often—Jadyn had been the one in band, while Kelsey had chosen to take orchestra—but that hadn't stopped Kelsey from harboring a secret crush on Bryce all through tenth grade.

"Of course. It's so good to see you again." Kelsey wrapped her arms tightly around herself, feeling her cheeks grow warm. Why hadn't she worn a jacket? Oh yeah—ninety degree weather. But the matching Batman T-shirt and pajama bottoms were just embarrassing.

"I can't believe it's you." He laughed, motioning to her ear. "At first I thought you might be Kelsey, but then I saw the tattoo."

Kelsey's hand flew to the spot. Her hair, pulled back in a high ponytail, left the tattoo exposed. The tattoo that she'd made sure was a perfect replica of Jadyn's. "Bryce, listen—"

But he spoke at the same time, cutting her off. "Did your parents ever forgive you for getting that tattoo? You always were a risk taker."

Yup, he was definitely thinking of Jadyn. She'd often teased Kelsey for being scared of her own shadow. Kelsey tried again. How had Bryce not already heard the news? "Yeah, about that..."

But Bryce seemed lost in a world of his own, caught up in memories from a decade earlier. "You know, I always meant to ask you out in high school."

Kelsey's heart stuttered painfully. Of course he'd had a crush on Jadyn. Every red-blooded male in their high school had been in love with her. Jadyn had been the bubbly, outgoing twin, up for any challenge. Like cliff diving in Hawaii, then getting caught in a riptide and drowning.

She missed Jadyn so much.

"I promised myself if I ever saw you again, I'd ask you out."

Well crap. Bryce's gunmetal blue eyes practically sparkled with joy at seeing Jadyn again, and Kelsey really hated to dash his hopes. She shifted, her high-tops squeaking against the floor.

"Wow," Kelsey said. "I'm very flattered, of course."

Bryce ducked his chin, making a lock of hair the color of chocolate fall over his forehead. Adorable. The tips of his ears were glowing red in embarrassment, and she realized that asking Jadyn out hadn't been easy for him.

"Sorry," Bryce said. "I shouldn't have assumed that you're still single. Of course you have a boyfriend."

Kelsey's stomach flipped at his expression. This was getting out of hand, even if her sophomore self was fan-girling inside. "Actually, I don't. It's just that, well…"

Oh, her heart! His lowered eyes and slumped shoulders caused Kelsey physical pain, sending tiny twinges that radiated out from her heart. How had Jadyn dealt with this kind of thing? Guys had asked her out all the time, and she'd never had a problem turning them down.

Kelsey was pretty sure that if she yanked Bryce's soul out of his body and jumped on it with stilettos, he couldn't look more disappointed. The poor guy was clearly crushed.

What would it hurt if she pretended to be Jadyn for just one night?

Kelsey immediately rejected the idea. She couldn't impersonate her dead sister—that was sick and twisted. If Jadyn were still alive, Kelsey *might* have considered it. Switching places had been a common occurrence, even as adults. Jadyn had been a jokester like that.

But no. Just no.

"Forget I mentioned anything," Bryce said quickly. She could see the shy Bryce from high school reappearing—the one who'd hidden behind his trombone and plumed shako hat. "I should probably get home. It was good seeing you again, Jadyn."

The smile on his lips showed no teeth, the clench of his jaw making the grin look forced. His eyes were sad, but he seemed to be trying hard to hide his humiliation. He'd probably go home and tell all of his friends what a jerk Jadyn Wilkes had turned out to be.

Kelsey squeezed her eyes tightly shut. She couldn't let someone speak ill of Jadyn. Couldn't let Bryce leave here crushed.

Really, what was the harm in letting Bryce go on a date with Jadyn? It was one evening, and a tiny white lie meant to help. It might even be sort of nostalgic—a brief, tangible connection with the twin sister Kelsey so desperately missed.

She could go on the date and be intentionally boring. After a painfully dull evening, Bryce would go on his merry way, content his life was complete without Jadyn in it. Wouldn't that be kinder than telling him the truth? Kelsey knew just how painful it could be to live life with unanswerable "what ifs."

If she went out with him, he'd stop looking at her like she'd used his heart for target practice. Living out her high school fantasy of dating Bryce was simply a bonus.

"Bryce, wait," Kelsey said. He was nearly halfway down the aisle now, and she realized she'd been lost in her thoughts for far too long.

He turned back around, his eyes wide with a hope that made Kelsey's own heart soar. She could do this. No biggie.

Kelsey folded her arms tighter around her waist, mostly obscuring the Batman logo on her pajama top. She wished she could tell Jadyn about this. Her sister would have died of laughter. Kelsey nearly chuckled at her own morbid word choice, then realized Bryce was still looking at her expectantly.

She lifted her chin, cheeks burning in a very un-Jadyn-like way. "I would love to go out with you, if the offer is still on the table."

"Definitely." Bryce took a few more steps cautiously toward her. "You are single, then?"

"I'm very single." So was Jadyn, probably. Could you date in heaven? If so, then Kelsey had no doubt her sister had found the hunkiest Roman soldier and promptly stolen his heart.

"Awesome." A dimple appeared in one of Bryce's cheeks, and Kelsey was struck with the insane urge to caress it with her index finger. She curled her hands into fists to stop the impulse. "How about Friday evening?"

An immediate and enthusiastic *yes!* was on the tip of Kelsey's tongue, but she stopped herself. Wedding planning was a weekend job, and she couldn't abandon a bride just because her high school crush asked out her dead sister. She knew for a fact it was the first weekend in months she didn't have a wedding to oversee, but couldn't remember if there were any dress fittings or menu tastings scheduled instead.

"Let me check my calendar." Kelsey gave a smile that she hoped held even a glimmer of Jadyn's confidence.

Her hands went to her pockets, searching for her phone, and encountered soft cotton. Crap. These pajama pants didn't have pockets, and she just now remembered that she'd stuffed her phone in her bra.

Kelsey turned away, trying to shield Bryce's view with her shoulder. She quickly pulled her cell phone out of her shirt, her entire body warm with embarrassment. Why was she always so awkward?

She pulled up her calendar, seeing a full day of appointments. But the evening was a big fat blank. She bit her lip, trying to hide her excitement. Jadyn wasn't the type to squeal over a date. Guys had practically kicked in her door for the mere chance at a grabbing a coffee together, so going out had never been a big deal to Jadyn.

Kelsey wiggled her phone, a small grin escaping. "Looks like I'm free."

Bryce grinned too. "Great. Let me get your number."

He held out his phone, and Kelsey took it. His screen was cracked, the spiderwebs making the display nearly unreadable. How old was that thing? But they exchanged contact info, and Bryce put his phone back in his pocket.

"Is seven okay?" Bryce asked. "I'd love to pick you up, if you're comfortable with that."

"That sounds great." Kelsey's inner romantic was totally swooning at his thoughtful consideration of her feelings. "I'll text you the address. See you then."

"I look forward to it." Bryce laughed. "It's so good to see you again, Jadyn. Today's my lucky day."

"Mine too." Kelsey's stomach twisted into a bundle of nerves. Already she was regretting her rash deception. Jadyn was the impulsive twin, not Kelsey. Well, except for the tattoo—she'd passed by a parlor a few days after the memorial service, and the next thing she knew, she was showing the artist a picture of Jadyn's and asking for the same thing. And, okay, pulling the phone out of her bra had been a little impulsive. But she'd only done that because she'd been caught off guard.

"I'll see you on Friday, then," Bryce said.

He pulled her into another hug. This time Kelsey allowed herself to savor it. His arms were strong, just like she'd always imagined them to be, and he smelled like apple cider. Kelsey slowly wrapped her arms around him, hugging him back. For reasons that made no sense, her eyes began to sting with tears, and she quickly blinked them back.

"I'll text you sometime this week," Bryce said, pulling away.

"I'd like that."

"Bye, Jadyn." Bryce gave her a crooked grin and sauntered away, his shoulders straight and walk confident once more.

Kelsey leaned against the doors of the freezer section, her heart thundering in her chest. Had she really just agreed to a date with her high school crush while impersonating her sister? In her Batman pajamas? She must be insane.

Kelsey turned around and grabbed a carton of double fudge brownie ice cream. Jasmine was never going to believe this.

But as Kelsey waited in line to pay, she couldn't help thinking that, insane or not, this was the most she'd looked forward to a Friday night in a really long time.

Chapter Two

Back in junior high, there had been a blue-eyed, spiky-haired boy. Kelsey honestly couldn't remember his name anymore, just that he'd been on the swim team, and both she and Jadyn had been twitterpated with him. Their crush had been especially obvious when he dove gracefully into the lane between theirs at practice.

It had only taken a month into the new school year for Kelsey and Jadyn to start bickering over the boy. He'd walked Kelsey to class, but eaten lunch with Jadyn. By Halloween, the argument had turned into a full-on fight, and Kelsey and Jadyn spent nearly a week avoiding each other. Not an easy feat considering they shared a few classes and a bedroom.

Kelsey had been the first to break down and apologize. They'd tearfully hugged, vowing to never let a boy come between them again.

That's when they'd created The Pact—the one that made a boy one hundred percent off limits if they both liked him. It was the only fair way to handle the situation and preserve their relationship.

Kelsey chewed on a nail as she waited at a red stoplight. Back in high school, she'd been disappointed when Jadyn voiced a preference for Bryce. Kelsey had admitted to liking him too, and they'd both stayed true to The Pact. It had only taken a few weeks for Jadyn to develop a crush on someone else, but Kelsey had silently mourned when Bryce moved away the next year.

And now Kelsey had a date with him.

The light turned green and Kelsey eased her foot onto the gas, turning into her apartment parking lot. A date with Bryce. She shook her head. That was the last thing she'd expected tonight. And she had to wonder... was agreeing to the date still a violation of The Pact? She and Jadyn had never discussed the finer points of their agreement, like whether death nullified it. And whether you were breaking it if, while on the date with the boy you both liked, you were pretending to be the other twin.

Kelsey killed the engine and grabbed her carton of ice cream. She trudged up the steps to her apartment, convincing herself it was totally fine. Jadyn wouldn't want Bryce to live with regret, so this date with Bryce was a good thing. She'd be so boring that Bryce would wish he could watch paint dry instead, effectively curing him of his schoolboy crush. With any luck, he'd be equally dull. This was the very definition of a win-win situation. Probably.

She kicked the door shut behind her and set the ice cream on the counter, quickly sending Jasmine a text. **Ready for Eye in the Sky?**

Just got home from work. Be over as soon as I change.

Kelsey grinned, pulling two bowls out of the cupboard and dishing them both a generous portion of ice cream.

A date. She hadn't been on a date in ... well, too long. A year, maybe? Jadyn had usually been the one to set Kelsey up, and she'd only been asked out once or twice since the memorial service.

Maybe Jasmine would let her raid her closet for something to wear, since all of Kelsey's own clothes screamed "business lunch." Not exactly the vibe she wanted to broadcast.

Wait. Maybe it was. She was supposed to repel Bryce, not attract him, for both their sakes. Nothing sucked more than the pang of regret. She learned that all too well after Jadyn drowned.

A knock sounded at the front door, and Kelsey called, "Come in!"

Jasmine slipped inside, managing to look like she'd stepped out of a magazine in high-waisted yellow silk pajama pants that flowed over curves Kelsey envied. The yellow set off Jasmine's dark skin, and her ebony hair was pulled up in a high ponytail that managed to look elegant instead of messy like Kelsey's.

"Sorry I'm late." Jasmine flopped onto the couch, tucking her legs up underneath her. They'd met while working together on Jase and Cassidy's wedding—Jasmine worked for the dress designer—and had become fast friends, only to discover they also lived in the same apartment complex. Not too surprising, considering they worked in the same business park as well, which was only a five-minute drive away. Now they had standing hangouts three times a week, work permitting, to watch their favorite reality TV shows.

"Working on another wedding?" Kelsey asked.

Jasmine's eyes sparkled as she grabbed her ice cream, nestling the bowl in one hand. "We had a consultation with a very famous pop singer today, and Genevieve let me sit in on the meeting."

Kelsey leaned forward eagerly. "Who?"

"Can't say anything until the contract is signed. You know the drill."

Kelsey sighed, flopping back against the couch. "That's so unfair."

"You'll find out soon enough. She wants a quick wedding." Jasmine took a bite of ice cream, letting out a groan of appreciation. "How did the wedding go? Cassidy looked absolutely amazing in the pictures you sent me. That dress fit her like a glove."

"The bridesmaids looked great, too," Kelsey said, nudging Jasmine with her foot. She'd done most of the sewing on those, although it had been Genevieve's design. "They are an absolutely adorable couple. I think they'll be one of those celebrity couples that make it."

"I think so, too. They look so real in the tabloids, and Jase went on that Toujour cruise so you know he's got his head on straight."

Kelsey laughed, shaking her head. Jasmine's brother worked for Luke Ryder, who was married to the woman who ran the Los Angeles branch of Toujour.

She took a bite of her ice cream, anticipation bubbling inside until she couldn't hold it back any longer. "Something exciting happened to me tonight. Not at work, though."

"Oh?"

"I have a date."

"What?" Jasmine let out a squeal. "Why have you kept that quiet for the last five minutes? Who's the lucky guy?"

Kelsey bit her lip, but it didn't help—she knew she was grinning from ear to ear. "His name is Bryce Michaels."

"I don't even need to know what he looks like." Jasmine waved a hand through the air. "That's definitely a hot guy name."

Kelsey laughed. "Oh, he's definitely hot. Dark hair. Tall enough to be a basketball player. There's a dimple in one cheek that's just to die for."

"Oh man, he sounds amazing. How did you meet?"

"I ran into him at the grocery store." Kelsey blushed, looking down at her pajamas. "Yes, I was dressed like a hobo and buying ice cream. I'll never mock your fashion advice again."

Jasmine threw back her head and laughed. "I've told you to stop going out in public like that. You must've been a real temptress to secure a date while wearing Batman pajamas. Maybe I should try it."

Kelsey's gut twisted as reality settled in. What was she doing, sitting here giggling like she'd just secured a date? If he'd known she was Kelsey, he probably wouldn't even have wanted to spend a few minutes catching up in the grocery store aisle.

"Hey, what's wrong?" Jasmine asked, frowning. "You look like someone just stole your puppy."

Kelsey took a slow bite of ice cream, giving herself time to think. She barely tasted the rich chocolate and brownies. "We knew each other in high school. I had a huge crush on him."

"That doesn't sound so bad."

"No, I guess not." Kelsey pursed her lips, thinking of the way her heart had ached every time Bryce grinned at her. She'd always suspected he was just being nice—that she was invisible beside Jadyn—and tonight had confirmed that. "Bryce was in band. He played the trombone, and I thought it was pretty much the sexiest instrument in the entire world. I never wished so badly that I'd decided to play the clarinet instead of the violin."

Jasmine laughed. "A trombone is sexy?"

"Oh yeah. I went to every game our sophomore year just to watch him play. Jadyn thought I was there to support her, of course—she was in band, too. But really I was paying attention to Bryce."

"Ah. So you guys were friends in high school?"

Kelsey cocked her head to the side, considering. "We didn't run in the same crowds, but we would nod at each other in the hallway. One time we did a group project together for English, and we were lab partners in biology for a term." The only time in her life she'd been eager for homework. "He was really nice and did a lot of humanitarian work. He was always heading up food drives, that sort of thing."

"Kelsey, I'm so excited for you! Clearly he had a crush on you, too, or he wouldn't have asked you out."

If only. For a moment, Kelsey considered switching topics and not telling Jasmine the whole story. It was kind of humiliating, when you thought about it.

But she couldn't do it. She needed Jasmine's help to figure out how to survive this date. "Yeah, I'm pretty sure he didn't have a crush on me."

Jasmine raised one eyebrow. "Then why did he ask you out?"

"Because he thought I was Jadyn. That's who he had the crush on." Just saying the words was painful.

Jasmine dropped her spoon into her ice cream bowl with a clatter. "Dang. What did he say when you told him?"

Kelsey dragged her spoon through the melting ice cream, not meeting Jasmine's gaze. "I may or may not have neglected to clarify the situation."

"What? Kelsey, you have to tell him that Jadyn's gone."

"Why?" Kelsey demanded.

Jasmine crossed her arms and let out a loud sigh. "Seriously?"

"Listen, okay? Bryce has had a crush on Jadyn since high school. If I tell him Jadyn's dead, he'll be devastated. You should've seen his face when he thought Jadyn was turning him down. He was crushed, Jasmine. *Crushed*. I couldn't tell him she was dead." Okay, she could have told him. But she really hadn't wanted to.

"So you decided to be her?" Jasmine set her bowl on the coffee table,

13

shaking her head. "I can't even picture you having this conversation. You aren't the type of girl who impersonates her dead sister for a date."

"Hey, I didn't judge you for going out with the unemployed former taco cart owner who didn't know how to use deodorant."

"That was a setup!" Jasmine laughed, throwing the remote at Kelsey. She ducked, and it fell to the floor.

"Yeah, well, I couldn't take Bryce's sad puppy dog eyes. If I tell him, he'll think he's missed his chance with Jadyn and be all regretful."

"He did miss his chance."

"Yeah, but he doesn't know that. I'll go on the date, be pleasant but bland, and we'll never have to see each other again."

Jasmine shook her head, grabbing up her ice cream bowl once more. "You know this is going to end in disaster, right?"

"Not necessarily."

"Oh, come on. I can't believe he hasn't found out about her passing already. What happens when he tries to add Jadyn on social media?"

"Bryce isn't really a tech guy. He wasn't on social media much in high school." Which had made finding out about him extremely difficult. "You should have seen his phone. It was like ten years old and an inch from total destruction."

"Okay, well, what about when he runs into someone else from high school—someone who knows Jadyn's dead? What happens when he runs an internet search on her name and finds news articles from the accident? Or her obituary? It's kind of strange he hasn't heard already."

Kelsey took an angry bite of ice cream, wincing when she bit down too hard on the metal spoon. It was pretty odd that he didn't already know. Their graduating class had been huge, but Jadyn had been popular, and Kelsey had seen the article on the accident shared dozens of times on social media.

Dang it. Why did Jasmine have to be so freaking right? Bryce would find out about the accident eventually, and when he put two-and-two together, he'd think Kelsey was a complete jerk. Stupid Pop Rocks in her stomach, clouding her judgment. She should've told him about Jadyn at the grocery store. But she hadn't, and now things were about to get incredibly awkward.

"You've made your point," Kelsey said. "This sucks."

"So you're going to tell him?"

"Yeah, and now he's going to think I'm some weird, creepy girl who gets her jollies from stealing the identities of the dead." Kelsey shoved another large spoonful of ice cream in her mouth, blinking back tears. "I'm such an idiot. He's going to hate me."

"I don't think he'll hate you." Jasmine patted Kelsey's back, smiling sympathetically.

"How do you even deliver that kind of news?" Kelsey grabbed her phone, scrolling through the contacts to Bryce. Maybe she should text him the news. At least then she wouldn't have to deal with the awkwardness face to face.

Jasmine's hand clamped over Kelsey's. "What are you doing?"

"Texting him."

"No way. You can't text him this kind of news."

Kelsey's finger hovered over Bryce's name. Dang. Jasmine was right again. A "hey, by the way I'm Kelsey and Jadyn's been dead for almost two years" text probably wasn't the kindest way to inform Bryce his missed chance was gone forever.

"Should I call him?" Kelsey asked. She stared at Jasmine, willing her to catch the *please don't make me call him* vibes. "That doesn't really feel right either."

"Yeah, I don't think you should call him."

Kelsey dropped her phone back in her lap, her throat feeling tight. "Okay. Then I guess that leaves telling him in person."

"Ding-ding-ding." Jasmine waggled her spoon back and forth, emphasizing each word.

The Pop Rocks were back in Kelsey's stomach, only this time they were angry. "Oh my gosh. I have to tell him on our date. How did I let this happen?"

Jasmine sighed, her lips pursed in apology. "Want my advice?"

Kelsey nodded.

"Tell him at the beginning of the date, not the end, so he can leave if he wants to. That way he doesn't have to waste his money on your meal under false pretenses."

"Oh. My. Heck." Kelsey grabbed a throw pillow, burying her face in it. "This is going to be the most uncomfortable date in the history of the universe."

"Is it really a date anymore?"

Kelsey scowled. "Gee, thanks."

Jasmine shrugged. "Sorry, girl. But you got yourself into this mess. Now it's time for you to get yourself out."

Chapter Three

Bryce walked away from Jadyn on shaking legs, hardly able to believe his own forwardness.

He'd asked Jadyn Wilkes out.

He could still remember the first time he'd met Jadyn. Bryce had always been shy, and being the new kid in high school had only been slightly helped by the fact that he'd started at the beginning of the year instead of mid-term. Bryce had been hopeful that his family's never-ending string of moves was at its end, but it wasn't meant to be—they'd moved again at the end of the school year in his dad's never-ending quest for a better job.

Bryce had headed into English and sat down beside a pretty girl with long hair the color of milk chocolate. She sat near the back of the classroom, her hands clasped on her desk and hair covering half her face. She glanced over at him quickly, then straight ahead once again. Her hair shimmered with the movement, and he had the sudden urge to run his fingers through it.

"Hey," Bryce said. It took all of his courage to muster up that single word, and he immediately felt stupid for saying it.

"Hi," she said back, and he was surprised when she sounded nearly as timid as him.

They didn't say anything for the rest of class. She stayed quiet the entire hour, dutifully taking notes in a spiral notebook as the teacher outlined class expectations. But Bryce had taken strange comfort in that one interaction. He'd introduced himself to someone at this new school, and the rest of the day felt more manageable with that out of the way.

He looked for the girl at lunchtime, kicking himself for not asking her name, but didn't see her. Bryce ended up eating alone at the end of a busy table filled with kids wearing polo shirts and glasses. It hadn't been so bad—no one seemed to mind that he was there, and he could blend into the crowd. Band was next, and he'd been excitedly nervous for it.

When he'd walked into the band room, Bryce had seen the same girl across the room. His heart had fluttered happily in his chest to see a familiar face among all the intimidating ones.

She was surrounded by boys, all of them laughing and talking as though they hadn't seen each other in an eternity. The girl tossed her long hair over one shoulder, giving a flirtatious smile to one of the guys. He folded his arms in response, obviously attempting the casual bicep flex.

Bryce's heart sank. So she was popular. He wasn't sure why that surprised him—maybe because she'd been so quiet in English? But she was classically beautiful, and she'd been nice, if a little shy. It made sense others would like her.

Maybe she wasn't really shy, because right now she seemed the total opposite of quiet. Perhaps she just hadn't wanted to talk to him.

Bryce took a seat in the back corner of the room, hating his dad for making them move yet again. Who knew a career in sales would be so unstable? Bryce had finally, after almost three years, found a few good friends in their last town. He wondered if they were missing him today as much as he was missing them.

The teacher walked into the room then, skinny as a beanpole with a receding hairline and glasses that magnified his eyes.

"Settle down," he said, but in a good-natured way.

The kids all laughed, slowly making their way to chairs. Bryce took that as a good sign. It must mean that this teacher was nice and friendly.

Someone sat down beside Bryce. He glanced over, surprised to see the girl. Why had she chosen a seat beside him?

She smiled widely, showing neon green braces, and gave a little wave. "Hi. Are you new?"

"Uh, yeah." Bryce sat up straighter. Did she forget that they'd met earlier? "We just moved here from San Francisco."

"Cool. What instrument do you play?"

Bryce swallowed hard. He couldn't believe this beautiful, nice girl was talking to him. "The trombone."

She ran a hand through her hair, the motion casual and unhurried. "I always thought the trombone would be fun. I play the clarinet."

"Nice." He wasn't sure what else to say. Bryce had never been great around girls, and this one had him particularly tongue-tied.

"I'm Jadyn, by the way."

"Bryce. I think we met earlier." He immediately regretted his words —why had he said them? Clearly Jadyn didn't remember their brief exchange in English that morning.

"No, I'm pretty sure we didn't. I'd for sure remember a cutie like you."

Heat crept up his neck, and Bryce hoped she hadn't noticed his blush. "You don't have English first period?"

She shook her head, smiling wider. "No, but my twin sister Kelsey does. I bet that's who you met."

Twins. That actually made a lot of sense, now that Bryce thought about it. They looked the same, but their personalities were so different. He'd been so enamored by her hair that he hadn't noticed much else about the girls. They were probably wearing different shirts or something, but Bryce didn't really pay attention to that kind of thing.

"Well, I feel stupid."

Jadyn laughed, shaking her head. "Don't. We're identical, and even our friends have a hard time telling us apart until we start talking."

"That's got to be wild." Bryce tried to imagine not being recognized by even his closest friends—not that he had any, what with the frequent moves—and couldn't. "What's it like being a twin?"

"Awesome." Jadyn's smile was completely genuine, lighting up her entire face. It made her look even cuter. "Kelsey is my best friend. I couldn't imagine life without her."

A few days later, Jadyn had officially introduced Bryce to Kelsey.

They'd never hung out outside of school or anything, but Kelsey and Jadyn had always been nice to Bryce—especially Jadyn. It quickly became obvious that Kelsey was indeed reserved, but Jadyn always greeted him like they were best buds. With every kind word and attempt to include him, Bryce's crush on her had grown.

He'd worried that sophomore year of high school would be a total disaster. But Jadyn's kindness had made it enjoyable, and in the end, he'd been sad to move once again at the end of the year.

He'd always regretted not asking Jadyn out. Always wondered if she would have said yes, even though she was way out of his league. To this day, he couldn't remember ever having a bigger crush on someone.

In high school, she may have been the outgoing, popular girl that Bryce knew he had zero chance of ever getting. He'd been shy and awkward, hardly able to speak to a girl without turning into a bumbling mess.

But he'd changed since high school. After college, he'd spent a year interning with a nonprofit before taking a paying position with the same organization and spending two years in South Africa, working on an animal reserve as he helped with conservation efforts.

Those two years had given him a confidence he'd always lacked, along with a pocketful of regrets for the opportunities he'd been too scared to grab. When he returned to the States last month, he'd vowed to take more risks and live life to the fullest.

When he'd seen Jadyn standing in that grocery store aisle, he'd known he had to prove to himself that he'd changed.

He couldn't believe she'd said yes.

Bryce was still thinking about Jadyn when he got to work Monday morning. He was tempted to text her and say just that, but it seemed forward, and maybe a little cheesy, so he deleted the text before he pushed send.

He arrived at Magnolia Gardens to find the decorators already hard at work, putting on the finishing touches on the new event center.

"Looking good," Bryce complimented them. "Think it'll be another late night?"

"Probably," the head decorator said cheerfully. "But we're on track to have everything ready by the open house on Monday."

"Excellent." Bryce grinned. He'd never worked for an event center before, but at the end of the day, marketing was marketing, and he was excited for the new challenge that Magnolia Gardens presented.

The new event coordinator wouldn't start for another few days, so Bryce handled the phone calls and scheduled two more events for the center. They were already almost forty percent booked for the next six months, which he considered fantastic considering they hadn't even officially opened. He was especially excited about his plan to feature a few different events in a new marketing campaign, and he really hoped he'd find the perfect couple to represent the wedding side of the venue soon.

But first, he had to plan the perfect date with Jadyn.

Chapter Four

J adyn had always been the type of girl who chose the perfect outfit for every occasion. She'd never stressed over what to wear on dates, because she knew what to wear before the invitation was fully issued.

Kelsey threw aside a matronly dress with a Peter Pan collar, sighing in disgust. If she'd ever wondered whether she possessed Jadyn's talent for fashion, well, this left no doubt. No wonder Jasmine was always shaking her head in hopeless dismay at Kelsey's wardrobe choices.

She thought longingly of the uniforms they'd been forced to wear throughout elementary school. Everyone had complained, but Kelsey had secretly loved them. Then junior high hit, and she could only be grateful that Jadyn allowed her access to her vast and stylish closet. She'd always told Kelsey when she looked amazing, and when she was in danger of becoming a social pariah. Being Jadyn's twin was a bit like having her own personal stylist.

Since Jadyn's death, Kelsey kind of wished she could go back to uniforms.

A floral blouse and a pair of pleated dress slacks joined the growing pile of clothes she'd ruled out. What exactly did someone wear on a date where they'd assumed the identity of their deceased identical twin? She flipped through her closet for the thousandth time. Yup, still stocked with nothing but power suits in varying shades of brown, blue, and beige. Well, and her Doctor Who and Batman pajamas, along with a few t-shirts emblazoned with her favorite Marvel characters. Captain America was so handsome.

Kelsey gritted her teeth. Darn her stupid job. Wedding planners—especially young ones—were supposed to look professional, not alluring, and Kelsey was more than willing to play the game if it helped her get ahead in her career. So far, her strategy had been paying off.

But that was before she was dressing for a date with Bryce Michaels.

Kelsey picked up her phone, staring at Jasmine's text from more than an hour ago. **Want some help getting ready for your date?**

She should have accepted her help immediately. Who was she kidding? Kelsey couldn't do this alone. She took a deep breath, then texted back. **Yes, please. Be there in a second.**

Jasmine opened the door before Kelsey could knock, smirking. "Finally decided to swallow your pride and ask for some help?"

"It's not like I'm going to find anything of yours I can fit into." Kelsey ran a hand through her hair with a groan. "You're like six inches shorter than me and actually have boobs."

Jasmine rolled her eyes, leading Kelsey into her spare room—make that her closet. The first time Kelsey had seen the space, her eyes had almost fallen out of her head. One entire wall held nothing but shoes and purses, while the other three were filled with racks of clothes.

"Have a look around," Jasmine said easily.

"What, you aren't going to offer suggestions?"

Jasmine leaned against the doorway, folding her arms. "I'll let you look first. You'll be more comfortable if it's something you want to wear."

"I don't think anything can make me feel comfortable on this date. I'm such a hopeless mess." Kelsey slid the hangers along the rod, only seeing how beautiful Jasmine looked in each piece. "Is this the type of date I should wear black for? I don't know if that's morbid. But if I wear bright colors, will he think I'm being callous about Jadyn's death? I mean, it's been two years. But I still miss her."

"You're over-thinking this."

Kelsey bit her lip, turning to face Jasmine. "I'm telling Bryce I pretended to be my dead sister. I don't think it's possible to over-think this."

"Okay, okay. I'll tell you what to wear." Jasmine grabbed a flowing skirt in a deep turquoise and a white wrap top, handing them to Kelsey. "Here, try these on. I've got some cute wedge sandals that I think you can squeeze into. They'll go perfect with it."

Ten minutes later, Kelsey was admiring herself in the full-length mirror. The skirt, which was calf-length on Jasmine, barely hit Kelsey's knees. She didn't fill out the blouse quite as well as Jasmine, either, but somehow it had accomplished the impossible and made her look like she had a waist. Overall, the outfit managed to look subdued while still showing some personality.

Not that Bryce would notice or care. At least, not after she told him she wasn't Jadyn.

"Jadyn would never have worn this." Kelsey picked an invisible piece of lint off her blouse, grief momentarily stealing her breath. "Maybe Bryce will notice and call me out."

"Guys never notice those types of things." Jasmine gave Kelsey a sad smile. "What would Jadyn have worn?"

An image of Jadyn on their twenty-first birthday filled Kelsey's head, and she had to smile. "Something much more daring, like stilettos and a tight party dress with a crisscross back. She had a knack for dressing sexy without crossing over the line. Her favorite accessory was oversized earrings. My lobes always hurt just looking at them."

"A girl after my own heart." Jasmine pointed to her own dangly earrings and laughed. "I wish I could've met her. Something tells me we would have gotten along great."

"You would have loved her." Kelsey blinked quickly, taking a deep breath. "Okay, now that I've swallowed my pride, are you up for helping me with my hair and makeup? Because I'm probably even worse with that than with fashion."

"Of course." Jasmine motioned to a chair in front of the vanity with a large mirror. "My sister-in-law, Zoey, has taught me a thing or two. Sit down, Cinderella. Let's get you ready for the ball."

Thirty minutes later, Jasmine declared Kelsey perfect.

"You're a miracle worker," Kelsey said, admiring herself in the full-length mirror. Her hair cascaded in soft waves around her shoulders, and Jasmine had applied Kelsey's makeup in a way that made her eyes look wide and innocent.

"Nah." Jasmine gave Kelsey a tight hug. "You're beautiful no matter what, Kels. Remember that tonight, okay?"

Kelsey's chest constricted as though a python had wrapped around her. "I'll try."

"Just tell him immediately, because it's only going to get more awkward as the night goes on. Are you sure you don't want me to come over for moral support?"

Kelsey bit her lip, then shook her head. "No, I think that will just make me even more nervous. But thank you for the offer."

"Call me tonight if you need to cry."

Kelsey nodded, walking toward the door. Jasmine hugged her one more time, and Kelsey tried to swallow back the fear coating her tongue.

"Good luck," Jasmine whispered.

As Kelsey walked back to her apartment, she couldn't help thinking that she'd need a lot more than luck tonight.

Like a giant hole in the earth to swallow her up.

Chapter Five

Kelsey barely had time to grab her clutch from her room and take a few deep, calming breaths before a knock sounded at the door.

"I can do this," she whispered, shaking out her hands. She'd take Jasmine's advice and tell Bryce immediately.

Kelsey threw open the door, ready to blurt out the truth. But her breath stuttered at the sight of Bryce, and all words fled from her mind.

He looked fantastic in a dark gray sport coat and a blue button-down shirt that matched his eyes. When he smiled, that dimple popped in his cheek, and Kelsey could almost feel her knees liquefying with happiness.

"Wow," Bryce said, his eyes glowing with an appreciation that had her entire body growing warm. "You look amazing."

He held out his arms, and she willingly walked into the hug. Kelsey could barely contain the shiver his touch evoked. It was all she could do to focus on his words.

"Thanks. You look great, too." She most definitely shouldn't stroke his dimple. Or his hair. That would be weird, right?

But man, she wanted to. Because if double fudge brownie ice cream was a person, it would be Bryce.

In high school, she had imagined this moment—their first date—a hundred times. But even her fantasies couldn't compete with this real-life version of Bryce.

Kelsey followed Bryce to his car in a daze, momentarily surprised when he held open the door to a dark blue sedan with shiny finishes instead of the rust-covered pickup truck he'd driven in high school. She slid into the car, running her hands over the soft leather seats.

"This is nice," Kelsey said.

"Thanks." Smooth jazz music floated from the speakers. Bryce's ears turned red, and he quickly switched to a Top 40 station. "Sorry, I meant to change that. Now you're going to think I'm an old man."

Kelsey laughed. She definitely wasn't thinking that. Bryce was classic. Timeless. Gorgeous.

He also thought he was on a date with Jadyn.

Crap. How had she gotten into the car without telling him the truth? Her super solid plan hadn't accounted for the fact that she could barely form a sentence around Bryce, especially when his dimple appeared.

Bryce pulled onto the road, one strong hand resting casually on the steering wheel.

She should tell him now.

A car whipped out onto the road right in front of them, and Bryce braked hard. Kelsey flew forward, the seatbelt catching her.

"Sorry." Bryce pointed to the *student driver* bumper sticker on the car. "Poor kid is probably getting an earful from his instructor right now."

Kelsey could only nod. Yeah, this definitely wasn't the kind of news she should deliver while driving. The date was likely to be a train wreck, but that didn't mean she needed to add an actual wreck to the evening.

She'd have to tell him once they arrived at the restaurant—preferably before they got out of the car, but after he'd come to a complete stop. The parking lot would probably be a good place to have a mostly private discussion.

He was going to hate her after tonight.

"So, have you kept in touch with anyone from high school?" Bryce asked.

"Not really." Obviously he hadn't either, or he would've heard about Jadyn's death. Where had he been the past few years that he'd never found out?

"Me neither," Bryce said. "But about three years ago I did hear that Mr. Thompson passed away."

"I heard that, too. It's so sad."

She should tell Bryce about Jadyn now. This was the perfect segue into the conversation, but he was still driving and the near fender-bender with the student driver had her on edge.

"He had to be pretty young. I'd be surprised if he was sixty." Bryce shook his head, full lips turned down in a sad frown. "He really was a great teacher."

Kelsey wouldn't know. He'd been Jadyn's algebra teacher, not hers.

Bryce continued to chat as they drove toward a nearby suburb that Kelsey knew had a lot of nice restaurants. She tried to keep up her end of the conversation, but from the concerned glances Bryce kept shooting her, she knew she'd failed abysmally.

He pulled up in front of a swanky restaurant, giving her an uneasy smile. "I hope you like Italian."

"I love it," Kelsey said. Jadyn had hated most Italian food, with the exception of spaghetti, but it was Kelsey's favorite.

Her door opened, and she looked at the proffered hand in surprise. A valet in a white suit jacket stood on the curb with a friendly smile.

She hadn't considered there'd be no parking lot.

Kelsey let the valet help her out of the car and watched as Bryce handed over the key. How was she supposed to tell him here? Kelsey had imagined sitting in the relative privacy of his safely parked car when telling him. Now she'd have to wait until they were in the restaurant.

Bryce gently rested a hand on Kelsey's back as he guided her through the front doors. Her stomach spasmed at his touch and her palms felt damp. As soon as they sat down, she'd tell him. Definitely before they ordered dinner.

Why hadn't she followed Jasmine's advice?

Soon they were seated at a table for two. It was tucked into an alcove, giving an intimate feel to the setting. Kelsey winced when she saw the three flickering candles serving as a centerpiece.

Bryce must have really liked Jadyn. This restaurant was posh, and it was evident from the crowded tables that he'd made a reservation.

"Are you okay?" Bryce asked, peering at her from over the top of his menu. "You seem a little distracted."

Kelsey set her own menu down, hands trembling.

She had to tell him. Now.

"I have been." Her voice shook embarrassingly. "I'm really sorry."

"Hard day at work?"

She'd spent most of the afternoon trying to calm down a freaked out bride. They'd done a final dress fitting, and it had brought up some anxieties and given the poor girl cold feet. But that was easy compared to this.

"There's actually something I have to tell you," Kelsey said. She really hoped he wouldn't hate her.

Bryce raised his eyebrow. "Okay."

"Bryce..."

There was no easy way to say this. Best to let it out, before she got lost in his eyes and forgot her purpose. Bryce picked up his water glass, taking a slow sip as though to fortify himself against whatever she was about to say.

"Jadyn died two years ago." Kelsey twisted a curl around one finger, holding her breath against the sudden wave of grief. It felt like two decades since she'd last laughed with Jadyn.

Bryce choked on the water, jerking back his hand. Water splashed down his front, drenching the front of his blue button-up.

Kelsey grabbed her cloth napkin, dumping the silverware onto the tabletop. Bryce took it, dabbing at his shirt without taking his wide and disbelieving eyes off of hers.

"Jadyn's dead? But then, that means..."

Too bad that hole hadn't opened up in the ground to swallow her. "Yeah. I'm Kelsey."

She waited for an angry explosion. One was definitely warranted. But Bryce just blinked, breaking eye contact.

"I should have told you at the grocery store. I'm so, so sorry that I didn't." Kelsey tripped over her words, rushing to defend her decision now that the truth was out. "Believe me, I tried. But you were so happy. Before I knew it, I was pretending to be her. That was wrong of me."

"How?"

"I mean, you were so excited to see her and every time I tried to talk, you—"

"No." Bryce shook his head quickly. "How did she die?"

Kelsey closed her eyes against the moisture, the corners of her heart still raw. She missed Jadyn so much. Relating the story never got easier. "A trip to Hawaii. She went cliff diving and got caught in a riptide." The Coast Guard had never found a body. Kelsey still had nightmares of Jadyn being eaten, still alive, by a shark.

Bryce leaned away from Kelsey, as though trying to escape. His fingers shook as he fiddled with the soggy napkin. "I don't know what to say."

Kelsey could think of a lot of names she deserved to be called right now, but Bryce was too much of a gentleman to use any of them.

The waitress appeared then, notepad in hand. "Are you ready to order?"

"I think we need a few more minutes," Bryce said, his voice tight.

The waitress glanced between them, as though just sensing the discomfort. "Of course, sir." She quickly walked away.

"We don't have to eat dinner," Kelsey said. "If you want to go home, I completely understand. My neighbor will pick me up." Jasmine had promised to be on standby in case such a need arose.

"No, let's eat." Bryce cleared his throat, pulling at the damp collar of his shirt. He wouldn't look at her and instead stared steadfast at a point just beyond her left ear. "I asked you on a date."

"You asked Jadyn," Kelsey reminded him.

"I guess I shouldn't have assumed you were Jadyn. But you have her tattoo." The tips of Bryce's ears glowed red and his voice shook. Kelsey wouldn't have noticed if she wasn't listening closely.

"I got that after she died. Red balloons were kind of our thing." Kelsey realized she was fiddling with her hair and quickly dropped it.

"You could have told me at the grocery store. About Jadyn, I mean." His tone was more confused than accusatory, and somehow that made Kelsey feel even worse.

"I didn't want to be the one to tell you she was gone. A lame excuse,

31

I know." Besides, then she wouldn't have had the pleasure of this humiliating evening. And what a shame that would have been.

She couldn't tell him the truth—that his stupid eyes and stupid dimple had kind of ruined her ability to reason.

Bryce cleared his throat. Nodded. "I didn't give you much of a chance to correct me. Of course I'm excited to see you again, too. I feel like I know you almost as well as I know Jadyn—*knew* Jadyn. She couldn't stop talking about you."

Kelsey's heart fluttered. Jadyn had talked about her, and Bryce remembered. But if there'd ever been a chance Bryce would like her, Kelsey had ruined it.

"Two years." Bryce ran his fingers through his hair. "I had no idea she was gone."

"I'm surprised you haven't heard about it."

"I've spent the last few years in South Africa working for a nonprofit. I just got back to the States a few months ago. Internet was spotty in most areas, and I'm not that great at keeping in touch with people, anyway." He ran a finger around the rim of his glass. "I would have liked to attend her funeral."

Kelsey opened her mouth to respond, but the waitress reappeared. Neither of them had looked over the menu, but Bryce ordered and so did Kelsey. She picked the cheapest item, even though it wasn't something she particularly liked. Bryce shouldn't have to pay for this date, but she knew he would. He was that kind of guy.

She should have told him about Jadyn over the phone.

"Wow. Gone." Bryce shook his head, as though struggling to accept this new reality.

The awkwardness overwhelmed Kelsey, like too much salt in a cookie. "I know."

"Not that I'm disappointed to be out with you." He stumbled over the words, as though he'd just realized the implied insult. "If I'd known you were Kelsey, I still would have asked you out."

Sure he would have. Was she supposed to find that flattering?

And now Bryce's eyes were suspiciously red. Fantastic.

"So ... tell me about your life," Bryce said.

"Oh." Kelsey blinked. She hadn't really planned for conversation after she dropped the bomb. "There's not much to tell."

"Have you been in California all these years?"

"Yeah."

"What about Jadyn—did she stay here, too?"

So that's how the night was going to go—fielding painful questions about Jadyn. "For the most part," Kelsey said, her words clipped. "She traveled a lot for work."

"What was she doing before she passed away?" The words were nearly a whisper. "Did she get to model like she wanted to?"

"A little." Where was the food? Kelsey had never wanted a date to end so badly.

The date nosedived after that. Kelsey tried her best to be friendly and polite through dinner. To Bryce's credit, he tried, too. But they couldn't shake the stiff awkwardness that hung in the air like a poisonous gas. He kept asking questions about Jadyn, all innocent enough, but each one was another fist to Kelsey's chest. Not only did it hurt to think of her twin, but it was obvious who Bryce wished he were on a date with.

He drove Kelsey home immediately after dinner. She silently hoped he'd stay in the car, but wasn't surprised when he got out to walk her to the door. The key slipped in the lock, and she felt her palms grow sweaty as she tried two more times before managing to unlock the apartment door.

"Thanks for dinner," Kelsey said, her hand on the doorknob and one foot inside the apartment.

"Sure." He didn't move in for the token end-of-date hug, instead giving an awkward wave. "Well, have a good night."

"You, too," Kelsey murmured.

But Bryce was already walking away. It didn't escape her notice that he hadn't promised to call. Not that she could blame him. Tonight had definitely stolen the number one spot on her personal list of worst dates ever.

As she kicked off the borrowed wedge sandals, her feet sighing in relief, Kelsey couldn't help thinking that at least tonight had accomplished one thing.

She was definitely over Bryce.

Chapter Six

Kelsey awoke the next morning to a text from Jasmine, wondering how the date had gone. Thirty minutes later, Kelsey was relaying the whole disastrous event while the two of them made chocolate chip pancakes for breakfast. Jasmine was sympathetic and kind, never once berating Kelsey for her stupidity, although Kelsey wouldn't have blamed her if she had. She knew she'd acted like an idiot.

But Kelsey had learned her lesson. Never again would she impersonate her sister. Two years without Jadyn, and a lifetime left.

The thought hurt more than almonds in ice cream.

Jasmine suggested an *Eye in the Sky* marathon, and Kelsey gratefully accepted her attempts to cheer her up. They re-watched one of their favorite seasons, where Tamera Hadley—who had recently married football star Wyatt James—had been dramatically stabbed in the back by none other than her ally, quarterback Drew Dempsey. But even a never-ending supply of ice cream and analyzing game play did little for Kelsey's mood.

Last night's date had hurt for reasons she wasn't sure she wanted to analyze. It went beyond missing Jadyn.

As Kelsey walked into work on Monday morning, she resolved to put Bryce far in the past where she wouldn't accidentally have to relive their humiliating date. Yeah, her love life was a total bust. And Jadyn, her other half, was gone. But Kelsey still had her job, and a day doing what she loved might be enough to finally erase the bad mood she'd been in since Friday night.

She sank into the swivel chair behind her clutter-free desk, waking up her computer. The room was small, so she'd taken a minimalistic approach to decorating to make it feel bigger. The black desk held only her computer, and behind her a bookcase hutch displayed a bridal bouquet and glass figurine of a couple in love, along with a few brochures from local wedding vendors. She'd gotten the office after Cassidy Erickson came to The Frosted Bride and, passing over all the more experienced wedding planners, had picked Kelsey to help plan her wedding to Hollywood heartthrob Jase Larson. She wondered if Cassidy had any idea what that had done for Kelsey's career. She'd forever love Cassidy for giving her that chance.

Kelsey loved everything about being a wedding planner—the romanticism, the coordinating of events, making brides' dreams come true. And today, she got to do a cake tasting with a Toujour bride. Who didn't love a job with cake?

Bryce was probably some boring accountant at a corporate firm where they didn't even eat cake to celebrate employee birthdays. She'd never gotten around to asking him about his job.

A knock sounded at the door, then it swung open. Her boss, Candice, looked as put together as ever. Her graying hair was sleeked back in a bun, and her suit jacket emphasized her hourglass figure. "Hey, Kelsey. Have a good weekend?"

Not really. But Candice wasn't the type of person who wanted honest answers to rhetorical questions. "Sure. What about you?"

"Hang on." Candice leaned out the door and muffled voices filtered through as she spoke to someone in the hallway. She straightened her jacket, focusing again on Kelsey. "Sorry about that. What were we talking about? Oh, right. My weekend was fine. I'm here because I need a favor."

Kelsey nodded, resting her arms on the desk. She wasn't surprised. Candice wasn't the type of boss who made time for small talk. "Of course. What can I do for you?"

"There's a new event center opening on 53rd Street called Magnolia Gardens. They're having an open house tonight for all the event planners in the area. Liz was supposed to go, but she called in sick. Can you go instead?"

Magnolia Gardens. Kelsey remembered Candice mentioning the new center some months back, but it was still under construction at the time. She quickly pulled up her calendar and saw that the evening was free. "Sure, I'd be happy to go. I don't have anything else scheduled for tonight."

"Perfect." Candice was already halfway out the door. "I'll forward you the information. Be ready to brief everyone on the new venue at tomorrow's meeting."

A new event center. Kelsey was still thinking about Magnolia Gardens when Candice's email arrived mere moments later. She scanned the digital invitation, but there wasn't a lot of information about the center. That was smart—it ensured people would actually come tonight to find out more. There would be a reception with refreshments, a brief presentation by the sales team, and a self-guided tour of the building and grounds. Kelsey had been to a few of these events before, and while they were a little dry, they weren't too painful.

Her day was filled with returning phone calls and answering emails she'd neglected while in Sunset Plains for Jase and Cassidy's wedding. Even though she'd been back a week, she was still trying to catch up. The high point of her day was the cake testing, where the bride and groom settled on an absolutely divine dark chocolate sponge cake with a raspberry ganache filling. The cake was almost good enough to make Kelsey forget about Bryce, who she most definitely wasn't thinking about anymore.

It was nearly seven o'clock when she drove up the tree-lined driveway to Magnolia Gardens. The trees were still in their infancy, but in a few years they'd frame the drive in a way that brides would love. An elegant building stood at the end of the drive, reminiscent of an English manor. Around the line of cars, Kelsey could just make out the circular driveway with the fountain in the center.

Her brides were going to love this place. She could already think of one or two brides who were planning weddings for late next summer that might be interested. Sunset bathed the building in a soft glow, and she imagined the photos that would be taken in the drive with the manor in the background. They'd be the kind of wedding pictures you printed as a sixteen-by-twenty canvas and hung over a fireplace mantle.

Kelsey pulled into the parking lot and got out, glancing up at the building. It had a regal feel, with dramatic archways and romantic pillars. Lanterns cast a soft glow across the walkway, and the gurgling fountain blocked out any sounds of traffic from the nearby road.

This place was amazing. She kind of wanted to get married here herself. Not that she was ever going to have the chance at the rate her love life was going.

Twenty-foot ceilings made the entryway feel grand and expensive, which Kelsey knew her clients would love. She caught sight of the curved staircase and instantly knew it would be a favorite spot for bouquet tosses.

Others lingered in the entryway as well, mostly women dressed in business attire. Kelsey smiled, nodding at a few she recognized. She accepted a glass of champagne from a passing waiter and made her way into the grand ballroom, keeping a mental tally of the building's features as she went. Impressive chandeliers. Romantic mood lighting. A large dance floor with room for a band. There was a shining black grand piano in one corner, where a tuxedoed man played soft classical music. The acoustics in this room were fantastic, and the music was clear without being overpowering.

"Kelsey?"

She whipped around, nearly dropped her glass of champagne. She'd been caught up in her thoughts and hadn't realized someone was behind her. Probably a vendor she'd worked with on some wedding in the past. After four years in the business, she knew most of them.

But it was Bryce who stood there, looking dangerously handsome in a black suit and blue shirt.

A shirt that was the exact same shade as the one he'd worn for their date last Friday.

So much for never seeing him again.

Kelsey's cheeks burned with a blush as heat made her hands feel sweaty. She clutched the champagne glass between them. Her heart was definitely not racing, but it wasn't exactly walking either. Bryce had managed to scare it into a light jog.

"What are you doing here?" Kelsey blurted. Smooth.

"I could ask you the same thing." Bryce motioned to the building. "I'm head of the sales and marketing department here. I'm assuming you're a vendor?"

"Wedding planner." Kelsey cleared her throat, searching desperately for something to say. She could not—would not—talk about their date. "This place is great. So eleful."

And she sounded like an idiot. Apparently her mind hadn't been able to make up whether the building was *elegant* or *beautiful,* and tried to say both words at once. Seriously, was what she'd done really so horrific that karma had deemed this an appropriate payback?

She quickly took a sip of her champagne, willing her nerves to calm. "Sorry. What I mean is, Magnolia Gardens is elegant *and* beautiful."

"Thank you. The marble floors were imported from Turkey, and the chandeliers are one of a kind. Each crystal was handpicked." He shoved his hands in his pockets, the tips of his ears growing adorably red. They'd done that in high school when he was embarrassed, too. "Sorry, old habits die hard. I didn't mean to give you a sales pitch."

"Don't worry about it." Kelsey took another sip of champagne. "So, um, how long have you worked here?"

"Only about a month. My boss at the nonprofit I worked for in South Africa helped me get the interview. His cousin owns Magnolia Gardens."

"That's nice."

Except it wasn't nice. It was a seriously unfortunate coincidence. Kelsey bit her lip, wishing again for that hole to open up and swallow her.

Why did he have to work here—the place where so many of her brides would be dying to start their happily ever afters? She had no idea how to create a working relationship with him after everything that had happened. Why had she ever thought lying to him was a good idea?

At least he was in sales. With a little luck, she'd be able to mostly avoid him. It wasn't like he was the event coordinator.

"Listen, Kelsey." Bryce's voice was low and husky, making the hairs on the back of her neck prickle. "I'm really sorry about Friday. I don't think I handled it all that well."

Kelsey held up a hand. She hadn't thought she could feel any worse about their date, but having Bryce apologize for it reduced her to the size of an ant. "We both apologized a thousand times on Friday. I feel like such an idiot for lying. I swear I'm not usually like that."

"I know you aren't." His very full lips quirked up in a grin. "I knew you in high school, too. Remember?"

She barely held back a shiver, not liking the way those words made her heart leap. "I remember." She glanced down at her champagne, watching the bubbles as she gathered her courage. "I'm probably asking the impossible here. But do you think we can forget that whole mess ever happened?"

Like maybe he could forget that he used to have a crush on Jadyn. Because Bryce in that suit? Her cheeks flushed, and she quickly focused again on her glass. Attractive didn't even begin to cover it.

Maybe she wasn't as over him as she'd told Jasmine she was.

"It is highly probable that the two of us will work together in the future," Bryce said. There was a smile in his voice, and she wasn't sure what to make of it.

"Right. So maybe we could just start over?"

"Starting over. I like the sound of that."

"Me, too." Kelsey held out her hand, then immediately wished she hadn't. It was probably gross and sweaty with nerves. Too late to turn back now. She was committed to this cheesy display. Awesome. "Hi, I'm Kelsey. I have an identical twin sister, but she passed away two years ago."

"I'm so sorry about your sister. My name is Bryce. It's nice to meet you, Kelsey."

His warm fingers wrapped around hers in a firm grip. Bryce grinned, and her insides crumbled at the dimple that appeared in his right cheek.

Kelsey was back in tenth grade with melting insides all over again.

What was happening? Friday had been a complete disaster. Ten minutes ago, she would've been happy to never see Bryce again. But the second he'd shown up, butterflies had spread their wings in her stomach and she'd become a giggling sophomore hoping he'd notice her.

But he liked Jadyn—not her. And now they were working together. Sort of. Besides, she and Jadyn had The Pact. Kelsey couldn't date him, even if she wanted to.

Bryce stuck his hands in his pockets, and that dimple popped in his cheek again as he grinned. "I'd better go get ready. I'm giving the first sales presentation in a few minutes."

"Oh, duh. Of course you are." Kelsey laughed, hating how nervous it sounded. "You're the sales guy. It makes sense that you're doing the sales presentation."

"Yeah, I guess so."

And now she didn't need to worry about dating him, because there was no way he was ever going to ask her out again. Not that she wanted him to.

Kelsey held back a sigh. She was being such a spaz. Jadyn had always known how to tone down that side of her.

"See you around." Bryce gave a small wave as he slowly backed away. Probably desperate to escape the crazy girl.

"Later, dude."

Bryce laughed, his shoulders shaking as he walked away. And what a view it was.

Dude? Kelsey threw back the rest of her champagne, then nearly choked as the bubbles tickled her throat.

As if their last encounter hadn't been humiliating enough, it seemed that her subconscious was determined to top it.

Chapter Seven

B ryce flipped on his apartment lights with a sigh. The night had been a smashing success, and he was confident that within the next couple of months Magnolia Gardens would be booked at nearly capacity for the coming year. Most of the vendors they'd invited to tonight's open house had sent at least one representative to attend— including The Frosted Bride.

He'd had no idea that Kelsey worked for them as a wedding planner, or that she'd be there tonight. Somehow, the career fit his image of her— organized, kind, always eager to help.

Seeing her again had been ... interesting. He'd left their date shocked and embarrassed. If he were being honest with himself, he'd also been upset with Kelsey for lying to him. It was still hard to believe that Jadyn —vivacious, enthusiastic Jadyn—was gone. Dead. Jumped off a cliff, caught by a riptide, and drowned.

But tonight, Bryce had remembered how much he'd always liked Kelsey. She'd been quieter than Jadyn—definitely the more reserved twin. Because of that, they hadn't interacted nearly as much. But Bryce realized that was because he and Kelsey were a lot like each other. They were both introverted and a little shy. He'd guess she often struggled with social situations, just like he did.

Bryce got ready for bed, still thinking about Kelsey. They'd been lab partners in biology and had spent almost every afternoon together for nearly three weeks working on their three-dimensional model of an animal cell. At the time, he'd thought he was developing a crush on Kelsey. But she'd never shown interest, and Jadyn had, so his attention had shifted.

Kelsey had suggested they meet at her house to work on the term project, and Bryce had agreed. His own home always felt so empty and lonely. His father often didn't get home until after Bryce was already in bed for the night and typically left before he woke up in the morning. And his mom... Well, even when she was home instead of out with friends, she wasn't really there.

But Kelsey's home had been filled with a happy energy that seemed to light up the entire house.

Bryce had been nervous the first time he went over there. Their two-story home had freshly painted shutters and neatly manicured flowerbeds. The name *Wilkes* had been stenciled on the mailbox, faded red and yellow flowers surrounding the calligraphy. Even the earth-toned brick seemed warm and inviting.

His family's rental home was nice, too. Mom was high maintenance, and Dad was committed to funding her lifestyle, no matter how many schools Bryce went to as a result. But their rental home was cold somehow, too. Everything from the walls to the countertops was varying shades of gray, and somehow the whole building managed to be modern and chic while still lacking any sort of personality.

But Kelsey's home more than made up for what Bryce's lacked. As he walked up the cracked driveway, he saw handprints in the far corner of the cement—probably Kelsey and Jadyn's from years ago. A bag of soil lay forgotten next to the front door, an empty pot and trowel sitting beside it.

Bryce took a deep breath and knocked. Kelsey answered mere moments later, giving him a shy smile as she held open the door.

"Hey." She brushed her hair behind one ear, and he caught a whiff of her shampoo. He couldn't quite name the scent, but it was fresh and clean and nice. "Come in."

"Thanks."

Bryce inhaled deeply, the scent of chocolate chip cookies lingering on the air. Did Kelsey have the kind of mom who baked, or was that a candle? Humming floated down the hallway from where a kitchen might be. He'd heard rumors that there were moms who made cookies, but Bryce had figured that was just a pretty lie Hollywood liked to perpetuate.

"Want me to take off my shoes?" Bryce asked, pointing to the basket near the door. The rug covering the hardwood floors showed signs of being recently vacuumed, and he had a feeling that Kelsey's mom was the type who liked to keep things tidy.

Her cheeks turned pink as she gave a quick nod. "If you don't mind."

"No, of course not." He slipped out of his shoes, looking around the entryway. A collage of pictures ran up the stairs immediately in front of him. He swallowed back the envy. The pictures clearly said that this was a family who enjoyed spending time together, and they had photo books of memories to prove it.

"I thought we could work in here," Kelsey said as she stepped down into a living room right off the front entryway. The walls were covered in pale pink wallpaper dotted with little roses. An elegant creamy velvet couch sat along one wall, with two wingback chairs across from it and a dark wood coffee table in between.

"Sounds good," Bryce said, dropping his backpack to the floor.

"I thought we could brainstorm different mediums to make our cell out of today."

Kelsey sank onto the floor, ignoring the furniture, so Bryce did the same. He eased his legs underneath the coffee table, setting his binder and biology textbook on top.

"There's always papier-mâché," he suggested.

Kelsey tapped a pen against her own textbook, nodding. "It's a good idea."

"But?" Bryce pressed.

"Nothing." Kelsey's cheeks turned pink, and he couldn't help thinking how it made her look even prettier. She pressed her lips into a line, drawing his attention to just how full they were.

"I can tell you have an idea," Bryce said. "What is it? Maybe it'll be easier than papier-mâché."

"I don't know about easier." Kelsey took a deep breath, her cheeks puffing out. When she finally spoke, the words came out in a rush. "But I thought it might be kind of cool to do one out of old car parts. Nuts, bolts, that sort of thing. My dad owns a garage, so we'd have lots of access to free supplies."

Car parts? Bryce leaned forward, his interest in the project piqued. "That would actually be really cool. We should do it."

"Yeah?"

"Definitely."

Kelsey brushed a strand of hair behind one ear again, her eyes sparkling as she nodded. "Okay."

An older version of Kelsey and Jadyn bustled into the room, a plate of cookies in her hands. She had the same dark hair as her daughters, although a few streaks of gray were visible near the hairline. A flowery apron was tied around a thickening waist, but her smile was wide and inviting, just like Jadyn's.

"Sorry, didn't mean to interrupt. Just thought you two might be hungry." She set the plate down, wiping her hands on her apron. The delicious scent wafted over to Bryce, stronger than ever, and his mouth instantly started watering. "You must be Bryce. It's so nice to meet you. I'm Mrs. Wilkes, Kelsey's mom."

Bryce couldn't remember his mother ever introducing herself when he had friends over, let alone baking cookies. "Thanks for having me. The cookies smell delicious."

"Oh, aren't you the cutest? Anytime, dear. Don't want Kelsey's friends going hungry when they're here."

"Mom," Kelsey hissed, her face glowing with embarrassment.

"Sorry." Mrs. Wilkes waved her hands, backing out of the room. "I'll be back in just a second with some milk. Can I get you anything else, Bryce?"

"No, this is great, Mrs. Wilkes."

"Mom!" Kelsey said again.

"I'm going." Mrs. Wilkes held up her hands, disappearing up the two short steps to the entryway.

"Sorry about that," Kelsey said, grabbing a cookie. "Mom likes to hover."

"I think it's great," Bryce said as he reached for a cookie of his own. They were still warm and the gooey chocolate stuck to his fingers. He took a bite and closed his eyes in delight. When was the last time he'd eaten something this delicious?

It must be nice to have a mom who cared.

"So you really want to do the bolts thing?" Kelsey asked.

"Absolutely. No one else will think of it, and I bet Mr. Barker gives us an A on creativity alone."

"Okay." Kelsey flipped open her notebook, turning to a blank page. "Let's decide what we can use for the different parts and start diagramming it."

They got to work. Time flew by as they sketched and brainstormed. Mrs. Wilkes brought the promised glasses of milk, and Bryce couldn't remember the last time he'd had a more enjoyable afternoon, homework notwithstanding.

A door slammed shut near the back of the house, making the framed family picture on one wall rattle. Kelsey's concentration didn't break as she continued sketching their diagram, but Bryce's attention was split. Low murmurs floated into where they worked, then quickly escalated to angry rumbles. Jadyn and Mrs. Wilkes? Bryce knew Kelsey didn't have any other brothers or sisters, and the voices were too high to be a man's.

"It's just a tattoo, Mom!" Jadyn shrieked. Her voice was much louder this time, and unmistakable.

Kelsey's head flew up and her shoulders started to shake. "Oh no. She's in trouble this time."

"What's wrong?" Bryce asked, dread pooling in his stomach. Would Mrs. Wilkes hurt Jadyn? She seemed so nice.

That's when he realized that Kelsey was laughing. She rolled her eyes, lips turned up in a smirk. "Jadyn must have finally gotten that balloon tattoo. She's been talking about it for a year and I thought she might try to get one. I wonder how she convinced the tattoo parlor she was eighteen?"

Heavy stomps came down the hallway, and Bryce watched as Jadyn took the stairs two at a time.

"Jadyn, we're not done talking about this!" Mrs. Wilkes took the stairs at a slower pace, hurrying after her daughter. "Your father and I—"

The words cut off as a door slammed shut, the voices once more reduced to incomprehensible mumbles. Kelsey was already focused again on the diagram, seeming completely unconcerned.

"How much trouble is she in?" Bryce asked.

Kelsey shrugged. "She'll probably be grounded for a month. No friends, no technology except for school, that kind of thing. She wanted me to get a tattoo with her, but I said no way. I guess she thought I'd tattle if she told me she was going through with it."

"That's it?" Bryce said. "A month's grounding?"

Another shrug. "Mom and Dad never stay mad at us for long. I think, at the end of the day, they just want us to be happy. And I know it's silly, but red balloons really make me and Jadyn happy."

That day always stuck with Bryce. Kelsey had seemed so calm and peaceful, even in the midst of a broiling family argument. It had only made him even more intrigued by the Wilkes family, and by Jadyn and Kelsey specifically. As Kelsey remained aloof and Jadyn continued to be overly friendly, his brief crush on Kelsey had shifted to Jadyn and stayed. She was so energetic, and he'd always appreciated the way she included him at school.

But whereas Jadyn was Bryce's opposite, Kelsey was his equal. The two of them were similar in a lot of ways.

As Bryce finally drifted off to sleep with memories of the past, he realized something.

He was glad Kelsey was a wedding planner. Because that meant there was a good chance he'd see a lot more of her in the future.

Chapter Eight

Kelsey wasn't surprised to find Candice waiting for her when she arrived at the office on Tuesday morning. Candice cornered her in the hallway, eyebrows lifted expectantly.

"How was the reception?" Candice asked.

"Great," Kelsey lied. No sense telling her boss about the totally awkward—and unprofessional—encounter with Bryce. "They had a very nice presentation, and the building is beautiful. I think it's going to become a favorite venue for our clients. The location is convenient to the city, but they've landscaped it so that you still feel like you're away from everything."

Candice clasped her hands together, the faintest of smiles turning up the corners of her mouth. "Excellent. Think you can put together a presentation by our staff meeting this afternoon? I want everyone brought up to speed so we can start showcasing Magnolia Gardens to clients. It'll be nice to have somewhere that isn't booked out eighteen months in advance, at least for the time being."

"Of course," Kelsey said. "Not a problem."

Except it kind of was a problem. Because Kelsey had spent way more time remembering how Bryce's lips used to move against the mouthpiece of his trombone than she had spent listening to his presentation. Seeing him again last night had totally rattled her. The collision of worlds was bizarre.

Hopefully Magnolia Gardens' website had the information she needed, because there was no way she was calling Bryce to ask for a repeat presentation.

For once, the universe was on Kelsey's side. Magnolia Gardens had an excellent website, and it helped her remember enough of the presentation to put together a decent slide show for the staff meeting. Candice would be pleased, Kelsey wouldn't be embarrassed at work, and she didn't need to call Bryce. Win-win-win.

Except she kind of wished she had a reason to call Bryce.

Cheyenne, one of her newest brides, arrived to distract Kelsey from her thoughts. Cheyenne was petite, with a bubbly personality that made Kelsey love working with her. They were still in the beginning stages of planning, but Kelsey felt like she already had a handle on Cheyenne's likes and dislikes.

"How is the bride-to-be doing today?" Kelsey asked, giving Cheyenne a hug.

Cheyenne laughed, returning it enthusiastically. "Fantastic. We've picked a date!"

"I know. February twentieth." They sank into their chairs, and Kelsey pointed at her computer monitor. "It's right here in your file."

Cheyenne waved a hand through the air. "Yeah, we're not doing that anymore. February is such a dreary month. What I really want is a summer wedding, so we've picked August twelfth."

Kelsey nodded, clicking on the file to update it. Cheyenne wasn't the first client to change the date, and Kelsey wasn't really surprised at the switch. Cheyenne's energetic personality and bright tastes didn't mesh with a winter wedding. "The weather is usually beautiful that time of year, which means we can look at outdoor venues now, too. Fifteen months is plenty of time to make sure everything is picture perfect."

"No." Cheyenne shook her head, sending her blonde curls bobbing. "Not next year. I mean August twelfth of this year."

Kelsey's hand froze on the mouse, staring at Cheyenne. "Uh, that's in three months."

Cheyenne nodded. Some brides lost that rosy glow while planning the wedding, giving themselves over to the stress of the event, but Kelsey had a feeling that Cheyenne wouldn't. "Zach received new orders from the navy. They're transferring him to Italy in September."

Kelsey leaned back in her chair, blowing out a breath. "Whoa."

"I know. We want to get married before we move. Not everyone can afford to travel, and we want all of our friends and family there to celebrate with us. Besides, I wouldn't even know how to go about planning a wedding in Italy. And there's no way he'll get enough leave to come back to the U.S. for a wedding here—not if we want a honeymoon, too."

Three months. Kelsey had thought planning an intimate Oklahoma wedding for a Hollywood megastar had been hard, but at least she'd had nine months for that. This was going to be a challenge.

"So can we make it happen?" Cheyenne asked.

"Oh, we'll make it happen," Kelsey said, hoping she sounded more confident than she felt. "The tight timeline will limit our options quite a bit, but we can make it work."

Cheyenne clasped her hands together with a squeal. "I knew you could do it."

Kelsey really hoped Cheyenne's trust wasn't misplaced. "We'll have to work fast. Our top priority needs to be securing a venue. I know you loved Rose Cottage, but they're usually booked a year out and I'm ninety-nine percent sure they won't have any availability this close to August. Not unless someone has just canceled."

Cheyenne lifted one of her thin shoulders in a shrug. "I like Rose Cottage, but Zach isn't a fan. What are our other options?"

Kelsey swiveled in her chair, reaching for some pamphlets. "The courthouse is absolutely gorgeous, and I think it would look especially regal since Zach will be in uniform. There's also Biltmore House, but it's almost an hour away from the city in good traffic—I know that's a bit further than you wanted. And last year I did an intimate ceremony at a city park that turned out absolutely beautiful. It's really secluded, and the scenery makes for a stunning backdrop. Those are probably our best options this late in the game."

Cheyenne pursed her lips, pulling forward the pamphlet for Biltmore House. "What about that new place on 53rd? We drove by it last week, and it looks almost ready to open. Zach absolutely loves the outside of that building. It's kind of got a European flair, which is absolutely perfect now with the move."

Kelsey swallowed, her heart beating a little harder than before. "You're talking about Magnolia Gardens."

"Is that what it's called?" Cheyenne dropped the pamphlet back to the table with a happy sigh. "Oh, I absolutely love that name. It would definitely look elegant on the invitations."

"It's a pretty name," Kelsey agreed.

"So is it open, then? Have you been inside?"

"Yeah. I was there last night, in fact. I think you'd like it." Kelsey couldn't decide whether that was a good or bad thing. Did she want to see Bryce again? Their last two encounters had been beyond uncomfortable, but she still felt all fluttery when he was around. "They're opening next month."

Cheyenne bounced in her chair, grinning so wide Kelsey could count every one of her teeth. "This is perfect! I mean, if they just opened they shouldn't already be booked, right? It's really conveniently located for all of our guests, and if it's brand new, it must be really nice."

"Don't get your hopes up just yet." Kelsey stifled a sigh at Cheyenne's hopeful expression as she reached for the telephone receiver. "New places are always really popular and tend to fill up fast, but I'll call and ask."

"They're going to have an opening," Cheyenne said confidently. "You mark my words. This is fate."

Fate. Karma. An eternal punishment from which Kelsey would never escape. She would absolutely die of embarrassment if Cheyenne found out that Kelsey had pretended to be Jadyn to go on a date with Bryce. Not that he'd tell anyone. Bryce wasn't the vindictive type—just something else she loved about him.

Kelsey gave Cheyenne a reassuring smile as the phone rang. Bryce had said last night that they were already nearly booked for summer. Was it wrong of Kelsey to hope that they wouldn't have an opening for August twelfth? Even if they did have an opening, that didn't mean she'd have to see Bryce. The event coordinator would be Kelsey's point of contact.

"Magnolia Gardens." The voice was deep, gruff, and unexpectedly masculine. Kelsey fumbled, nearly dropping the receiver. The voice sounded like ... well, like it might belong to Bryce. A coincidence, no doubt. She was pretty sure answering phones wasn't in his job description.

"Uh, hi." Kelsey blinked, trying to refocus. "This is Kelsey Wilkes from The Frosted Bride. I have a client who is interested in booking your venue."

"Kelsey?"

There was no mistaking his voice now. Her heart stuttered in her chest as warmth spread up her neck. Kelsey hoped Cheyenne couldn't see her blush. "Hey, Bryce. I didn't expect you to answer the phone."

"It's not really part of my job, but our scheduling coordinator doesn't start until next week and I offered to fill in for the time being."

Of course he did, because Bryce was just that nice of a guy. It was equal parts frustrating and adorable.

"Let me pull up the calendar. What day is your bride looking at?" Bryce asked.

Right. Cheyenne. The wedding. "August twelfth. I know that's only a few months away, but since you're so new we were hoping you weren't booked yet."

"Let's see..." She could hear Bryce typing on the keyboard, and it made her toes curl and heart speed up. "It looks like we do have some openings on that date. The Iris room is booked, but the Lily and Gardenia rooms are still available."

Cheyenne pointed her thumbs up, then down, clearly asking for news. Kelsey gave a thumbs up, and Cheyenne clapped her hands silently together, that wide smile stretching her cheeks again.

But all Kelsey could think about was that she was talking to Bryce Michaels on the phone. She'd fantasized about this moment a thousand times in high school. Living the dream felt fantastic and awful all at once, like chasing down chocolate cake with freshly squeezed lemonade.

"That's great news," Kelsey said. "Can we schedule a time to come by and do a tour?"

"Of course," Bryce said. "Name a date and time, and we can make it work."

"Let me check with the bride." Kelsey put a hand over the mouthpiece, her stomach full of butterflies. If Bryce was taking phone calls, he might be conducting tours right now, too. That seemed like something that might fall under the job title of *marketing director*. "They still have two rooms available on August twelfth. When do you want to go and take a look?"

"Ahh, I'm so excited!" Cheyenne let out another squeal. "Is tomorrow too soon? I'm off work at two."

Kelsey had no idea what her schedule looked like tomorrow, but she knew she'd have to rearrange it to make this appointment work. August twelfth would be here before they knew it, and they couldn't waste even a day of planning. She uncovered the mouthpiece and asked Bryce, "How about tomorrow afternoon?"

"I can do four o'clock," Bryce said.

"Four o'clock it is."

Kelsey clutched her phone tightly to her ear. She was going to throw up. Bryce had said *I can do four o'clock*. That meant he would give them the tour.

Cheyenne held up a hand for a high-five, and Kelsey weakly complied.

"I look forward to seeing you again, Kelsey," Bryce said. His voice slid over her like a warm ocean wave, making her shiver.

"See you tomorrow," Kelsey agreed. "Bye."

Cheyenne jumped out of her chair, trapping Kelsey's arms to her side in a fierce hug. "Oh my gosh, thank you! Zach is going to be so excited."

"Of course," Kelsey said. "I'm glad it's all working out."

"This is meant to be, Kelsey. I just know it. I can't wait to see Magnolia Gardens."

I look forward to seeing you again. Had Bryce meant that in the general sense, or in the I'm-secretly-in-love-with-you-and-will-be-eagerly-awaiting-your-arrival sense? Kelsey almost snorted, then forced herself to focus on Cheyenne. After what she'd done to Bryce, there was no way he'd ever like her romantically.

Which was totally and completely fine. Because Kelsey was definitely over her schoolgirl crush on Bryce Michaels.

Chapter Nine

Kelsey drove slowly toward Magnolia Gardens, her stomach curdling more than expired milk. With an entire night to obsess over seeing Bryce for the third time in less than a week, she'd convinced herself that she would once again come out of the encounter looking like a fool. She'd trip and fall, or stumble over her words, or bring up that awful date. And this time would be even more humiliating, because Cheyenne would be there to witness the disaster.

Kelsey did her best to stretch out the drive, not going so much as a mile over the speed limit. Despite her efforts, every light she hit was green. She also encountered almost no traffic along the way, which had to be some sort of record.

The slow driving did nothing to get Bryce out of her head. Why did she still care about his opinion, anyway? Sure, he had spent his Saturdays in high school playing the trombone at a retirement center. Yes, he'd been on the honor roll. He'd taken a girl with special needs to the winter formal because he knew she had a crush on him. He'd been a very sexy Doctor Who one year for Halloween.

But that was high school. She wasn't sixteen anymore, and neither was Bryce. A lot could happen in a decade, and for all she knew, maybe now he was a complete jerk.

Except he wasn't. Not even close. Because a jerk wouldn't have been nearly as nice about the lying-about-her-dead-sister thing. He wouldn't have sat through dinner and paid for her meal and walked her to the door.

Her stomach wriggled and squirmed with anxiety while her traitorous mind anticipated seeing him again. In high school, she'd considered him practically perfect. But the adult version of Bryce was even better.

Kelsey arrived at Magnolia Gardens ten minutes early thanks to the green traffic lights. She glanced up at the imposing building and pictured Bryce sitting at a desk somewhere inside, waiting for their arrival.

Maybe she should wait in the car for Cheyenne and Zach instead of going inside.

Kelsey rolled down her windows and nervously drummed her fingers against the steering wheel in time to the music. She and Bryce could both be professionals today. He had proven that much with how kind he'd been both at the reception and over the phone. And hadn't they agreed to forget the whole disastrous date and start over?

There was no reason why they couldn't put the past behind them and be friendly colleagues. Maybe even friends. Or more than friends.

No. They would be friendly colleagues—nothing more.

Zach and Cheyenne finally arrived, and they all walked into Magnolia Gardens together. Cheyenne sucked in her breath as she admired the entryway. Her eyes went right to the spiral staircase, just as Kelsey had known they would. The room seemed even bigger without guests crowding the space, and their footsteps on the marble floor echoed off the coffered ceiling.

"It's beautiful," Cheyenne breathed, wrapping both of her arms around one of Zach's. "I think I already love it."

"It's really nice," Zach agreed. He pointed to the chandelier. "That thing is massive."

"Very elegant," Cheyenne agreed. She motioned to the crown moldings. "I love the attention to detail."

Kelsey didn't interrupt, allowing the couple to explore the room without her input. She heard a door shut somewhere on the second floor, and Bryce appeared at the top of the stairs, looking impeccable in a suit and tie.

She pressed her hands to her quivering stomach, her knees trembling as that dimple made its appearance in one cheek. In high school, he'd mostly worn jeans and T-shirts. She tried to imagine what grownup Bryce would look like in such a casual outfit and nearly swooned.

"You must be Cheyenne and Zach," Bryce said, extending his hand toward both of them. Kelsey caught a whiff of his aftershave, something earthy with a hint of spice.

"That's us," Cheyenne said. "Magnolia Gardens is absolutely gorgeous. We only live a few miles away, so we've watched its progress during construction. It's even more beautiful than I imagined."

Bryce smiled. There went that dimple again, and with it Kelsey's brain.

"Thank you," Bryce said. "We had a fantastic architect and construction crew. We have three reception halls, each with their own private dance floor and outside garden space. I don't know how the architect managed it, but even if we have three events running simultaneously, it feels like you're the only party in the building."

"Sounds wonderful," Cheyenne gushed, looking up at Zach. "We both have a lot of friends and family, so it's going to be a pretty big wedding—maybe one hundred and fifty people."

"We can accommodate that," Bryce said easily. "The Gardenia room can comfortably hold up to two hundred and eighty and has an outside space as well which many opt to utilize as part of the reception area. Are you planning on having the wedding here as well, or will that be at a separate venue?"

"Everything will be at the same place," Kelsey said, and Cheyenne nodded in confirmation. "With the time crunch we're on, Cheyenne decided to not stress about trying to find a separate venue for the wedding."

"I can't imagine finding somewhere better than this anyway," Cheyenne said. "Are you giving us the grand tour?"

"Yeah, I'm afraid you're stuck with me today." Bryce's tone was joking, and Kelsey's stomach gave a happy leap at the confirmation that he'd be directing them today. "Our official grand opening isn't for another two weeks and we're running at about half-staff until then, so I'm filling in."

"Thanks again for letting us see this place early," Zach said. He grabbed Cheyenne's hand and squeezed. "We really want to get married before I'm transferred to Italy."

"Transferred?" Bryce asked.

"That's why we moved up the wedding date," Cheyenne said. "Zach is in the navy."

Bryce continued to ask Cheyenne and Zach questions about the wedding as he showed them the venue. Kelsey followed at the back of the group, struggling to pay attention to Bryce's words instead of how his lips looked while forming them. He had a quiet confidence about him that had been missing in high school. Back then he'd always been a little socially awkward, just like her, but now he conversed easily with Cheyenne and Zach.

They ended the tour back in the front entryway, right where they'd started.

"I'll give you two a few minutes to discuss things," Bryce said, smiling at Zach and Cheyenne.

Kelsey knew they wouldn't need a few minutes. She could already tell by the stars in Cheyenne's eyes that she was sold, and by the warm glow in Zach's that he'd give his bride anything she wanted.

"Kelsey, can I have a word with you?" Bryce asked.

She blinked, her focus drawn back to him. "Of course."

Cheyenne and Zach's heads were close together in whispered conversation, and they barely seemed to notice as Kelsey and Bryce moved a discreet distance away. He turned to face her, and she was suddenly aware of how closely they stood together. She bit her lip, gazing up into Bryce's eyes.

"I feel like a jerk," he said, his voice low and brows drawn together.

Well, that was unexpected. "Uh, why? I thought the tour went really well—"

He rubbed a hand over his jaw. "That's not what I mean. I mean, well, about Jadyn. About our date."

He might as well have dumped a bucket of ice water over her head.

58

Kelsey took a step back, folding her arms tightly. "We don't have to talk about that. I thought we agreed to start over."

"I know. But I can't stop thinking about it." He shook his head, his eyes sorrowful. "I was so caught up in my shock over Jadyn's death that I didn't even stop to think about how it has affected you. I can't imagine what it's like to lose your twin. How have you been?"

Kelsey blinked, suddenly fighting back tears. Losing her twin had felt like losing a part of her soul. But she was learning how to get by without Jadyn. She missed her, but not with the same breathless intensity she had for the year immediately following her death. "It's been hard. You know how vivacious and strong she always was. Everyone loved her. Sometimes I can't believe she's really gone."

"Everyone loved you in high school, too," Bryce said gently.

Kelsey snorted. She had always been *Jadyn's twin* in high school, and never simply *Kelsey*. It had been hard to figure out who she was without her sister.

"It's the truth," Bryce said. "I know we didn't really hang out back then or anything, but I always liked you."

The words made heat rush up Kelsey's spine. She hoped Bryce couldn't see her blushing. "I always liked you, too."

He grinned, making that dimple pop. "I know things have been a little awkward the last week, but do you think maybe we could try to be friends? Seems like we might be seeing a lot of each other in the future."

Kelsey squeezed her arms tighter around her waist, his words making her entire body fluttery. "I'd like that."

"Good. And if you ever need to talk about Jadyn, I'm here for you. You can call or text me anytime."

The words were right. But a thread of worry wound its way around Kelsey's heart, making her cautious. Did he really want to be friends? Or did he only want to talk about Jadyn?

Worse yet—did he want to use her as Jadyn's replacement? They did look exactly the same.

She shook her head, following Bryce back over to Zach and Cheyenne. She was being ridiculous. Bryce had paid for her meal after she lied to him. He'd done humanitarian work in South Africa, for heaven's sake. He was a textbook nice guy. And nice guys didn't do that.

"So, what do you think?" Bryce asked, clapping his hands together.

Cheyenne's face shone with excitement. "We love it! We can't wait to get married here."

Zach patted his pocket as though searching for a wallet, exaggerating the movements. "Where do I pay?"

They all chuckled.

"Let's get a contract drawn up for you guys," Bryce said. He glanced at Kelsey, then back at Cheyenne and Zach. "I do have one question for you first, though. Since we're just getting off the ground, we're hoping to closely observe the experiences of a few different events and use them for marketing purposes. If you're interested, I'd love to have you represent the wedding side of our venue. We'd be honored to have a military couple as part of the campaign. I can offer you a thirty percent discount on your event for the trouble."

Cheyenne's eyes flicked to Zach's, wide and excited. "What would we have to do?" she asked.

"Not much," Bryce said. "Let our photographer take a few pictures throughout the process. Maybe spend an hour or two answering questions in front of the camera. You'd sign a release giving us permission to use clips in promotional ads and campaigns. Mostly you just have to let us observe what you'd already be doing. I'd be there for you every step of the way."

Kelsey fiddled with her hair, focusing on Cheyenne and Zach. Would they accept? Panic battled with excitement, and she had no idea who she wanted to win. She loved the idea of spending more time with Bryce. But she was also terrified by it.

Did Bryce really want them to be friends?

"We accept," Zach said, and Cheyenne nodded eagerly. Kelsey let out a breath she hadn't even known she was holding.

"Fantastic." Bryce shook Cheyenne's and Zach's hands, but his eyes were locked on Kelsey's.

She was sixteen years old all over again. Could almost see the endless lines of *Mrs. Bryce Michaels* she'd doodled in her notebooks, then hidden so Jadyn wouldn't see them.

"Well, Miss Wilkes," Bryce said, finally holding out a hand to Kelsey.

"Looks like we'll be seeing a lot of each other over the next three months."

"Yeah." Kelsey let his strong hand envelop hers. Was it possible to have a heart attack from twitterpation? Because she seriously felt like she was going to pass out from his sheer closeness. "It looks like we will."

Chapter Ten

Bryce grabbed a shopping cart and headed into the grocery store, moving his neck back and forth to try to ease the ache from another long day spent at work. The rest of the staff should start next week, and he hoped then he could go home before eight o'clock at night.

Today he hadn't cared about the long hours, though. He'd gotten to spend two of those hours with Kelsey. She'd come by with Cheyenne to work up sketches of the room layout for the ceremony and reception. Bryce hadn't really needed to be there for it, and hadn't booked the camera crew for the mostly uninteresting appointment, but he'd still found himself making up an excuse to spend time with her.

Cheyenne hadn't seemed to mind Bryce's presence, and neither had Kelsey. As they discussed where they should set up the buffet tables and guest book, they'd asked Bryce for his opinion and seemed to value his answers. Kelsey had laughed and joked with Cheyenne, and Bryce had watched in amazement as she made the experience both easy and fun.

It had made Bryce realize how much he wanted someone to laugh with at the end of each day.

He hadn't dated much in high school. College had brought along a few girlfriends, but no one Bryce had wanted a serious relationship with.

And there hadn't been time to date while in South Africa. But meeting Kelsey again had reminded Bryce that maybe it was time to think about settling down.

The grocery store had that sleepy, late-night quality that Bryce had become accustomed to since moving back to California. The aisles were mostly empty, and the music turned down low. Without the sun streaming through the skylights, the store even seemed darker, like it was poorly lit.

Bryce nodded to a cashier and headed toward the produce department. He didn't mind the quick shopping trips at the end of long days. In fact, he sort of preferred them. It lessened the risk of running into random neighbors he'd have to make small talk with.

He perused the produce, passing over the green bananas and picking up a pineapple instead. One of these days he really should make a list. Maybe then he'd end up with food he could cook a meal from instead of a bunch of random ingredients. But he sniffed the pineapple, his mouth watering at the sweet scent, and added it to his cart. He'd eat it as a snack if he couldn't figure out a meal for it.

Bryce turned for the potatoes and froze. There, only a few feet away, was Kelsey.

She stood in front of the refrigerated section, head cocked to the side as she examined the bagged salads. Her warm brown hair was pulled back in a messy bun, exposing the red balloon tattoo behind one ear, but he would have recognized her even without that obvious giveaway. There was something about the tilt of her head, the way she rested her weight on one leg, that was decidedly Kelsey. She'd changed from the conservative green skirt and white sleeveless blouse she'd worn earlier in the day into frayed jean shorts and a baggy T-shirt that hung distractingly about her hips.

She turned, as though sensing his gaze. A batman logo was displayed prominently across the front of her shirt, and Bryce grinned. When he'd found her in her Batman pajamas last time they'd met at a grocery store, he'd thought he'd never seen something more adorable.

"Hey, Bryce," Kelsey said, lifting her hand in a tentative wave.

He pushed his cart toward her, his palms slipping on the handlebar.

"This is the second time we've run into each other here," Bryce said, making his tone light and teasing.

"We really should stop doing that," Kelsey agreed. Her laugh was low and made his stomach swarm with butterflies. No, not butterflies—moths. That was more manly.

"Are you a late night shopper by choice or by chance?" Bryce asked.

"Definitely by choice. I hate the weekend crowds, and I like sleep too much to come before work."

"Me too."

"So is this your weekly trip?" Kelsey asked.

"I don't plan meals out very well. Sometimes I come every day. Sometimes I don't come for two weeks."

"You sound like me."

There was that laugh again—Bryce liked it more every time he heard it.

She moved toward the frozen food aisle and Bryce followed, no longer caring about grocery shopping.

"Mind if I tag along while you shop?" Bryce asked. "Or we could awkwardly wave at each other every other aisle if you prefer."

Kelsey smirked. "I guess we can shop together. But no judging my food choices. I work a lot of late nights, and it's kind of a pain to cook just for one."

He wondered if she didn't have time for cooking, didn't like cooking, or didn't know how to cook. He seriously doubted the latter. Mrs. Wilkes seemed like the kind of mom who would make sure her kids knew their way around the kitchen. Maybe one day he could talk Kelsey into sharing a meal together. He imagined her in his small kitchen, a whisk in one hand as she stirred some sauce on the stove. She'd look good doing it, whatever the sauce tasted like.

"No judgment here," Bryce said. "I don't cook very often, either. Thank heavens for frozen food."

"We both shop late at night and avoid cooking. Geez, it's like we're the same person," Kelsey joked.

"Not the same person. We just have a lot in common."

"Yeah, I guess we do."

He tried not to admire Kelsey's long legs as she stepped forward, opening one of the freezer doors. A moment later, she tossed two frozen pizzas in her cart.

"Canadian bacon?" Bryce made a face and reached for his own frozen pizza—a pepperoni one. "Don't tell me you're one of those people who like pineapple on your pizza."

"As a matter of fact, I am." She lifted her chin, her lips turned up in a smirk. There was a sparkle in her eyes that he loved. He was used to the quiet and reserved Kelsey and liked this show of defiance. "In fact, I would argue it's the only way to enjoy pizza."

He put a hand to his chest theatrically, pleased when she laughed at his antics.

"You wound me," he said.

She motioned to his cart. "You obviously like pineapple."

"Yeah, but not on pizza. Fruit and tomato sauce don't mix."

Kelsey lifted her shoulders in a shrug. "You know, they say you learn a lot about a person when you grocery shop with them."

"And what are you learning about me?"

"That you have awful taste in pizza."

Bryce laughed loudly at that, his voice echoing off the empty aisles. Kelsey's cheeks turned pink at the sound, but she had a pleased smile on her lips, like she was glad he found her funny. He'd forgotten how entertaining she could be once she warmed up to someone.

They moved onto the bread aisle, where they both reached for the same honey wheat brand. Bryce held up his loaf in triumph.

"See?" he said, brandishing the bread. "I don't have bad taste in everything."

"This could be an anomaly." She pointed toward the bagels with a flourish. "Here's the real test—what bagels do you love?"

He pretended to study the bagels intently before finally reaching for a bag of blueberry. He held it up, loving the way her eyes sparkled with amusement. "Did I pass?"

"I guess I'll give it to you." She grabbed her own bag of bagels—chocolate chip, but the same brand as his blueberry.

"See? We're not so different after all," Bryce said.

"No, I guess we aren't."

They moved on to the deli aisle, where Bryce selected ham and Kelsey picked turkey. He loved watching her shop. It was so entirely normal, and seeing her in this setting made him like her even more.

"It's been fun working together the last few days," Bryce ventured. Had she noticed the way he made excuses to spend time with her when she was at Magnolia Gardens? He wasn't sure whether he wanted her to or not.

"Yeah, it has been." Kelsey's tone was easy and light, like she meant the words. "You couldn't have picked a better couple to use in your marketing campaign. Cheyenne and Zach are great."

"They've been everything I hoped for and more," Bryce agreed. They were kind of the perfect clients, and the fact their wedding was so soon was a definite bonus. Bryce didn't have a year to follow a couple before launching the marketing campaign. "Cheyenne loves everything, and Zach is so easygoing. I think they'll do really well around the cameras."

"I know I shouldn't have favorite clients, but I've really enjoyed working with those two," Kelsey agreed. "Their three-month timeline is a little stressful, but I think we'll pull it off, thanks to Magnolia Gardens."

Bryce would make certain that Zach and Cheyenne's wedding day was perfect. He wanted to show Kelsey how competent he was. How fun it would be to work together on future weddings.

"It's going to be great," Bryce agreed.

"Who would have thought, way back in high school, that we'd one day be working together in the wedding industry?"

Bryce thought back to those few weeks during their biology project when he'd harbored a secret crush on Kelsey. He'd thought a lot about her then—what it would be like to go to winter formal together, how fun it would be to sit close at lunch. But he couldn't say he'd ever thought of working together on a wedding, much less one that wasn't their own. "Life is kind of crazy."

"Yeah. It's definitely taken me places I never imagined."

Her voice was filled with sadness, and a pang of sorrow struck Bryce right in the heart. She must be thinking of Jadyn. He'd forgotten for a moment just how tough the last few years had been for Kelsey.

They moved on to the baking aisle. Kelsey grabbed a boxed brownie mix, while Bryce reached for a bag of flour. Neither of them spoke, but the silence wasn't uncomfortable. It felt so natural to shop with Kelsey. Like they'd been doing it their entire lives.

That image flashed into his mind again of the two of them cooking together. She'd smear whipped cream on his nose, and he'd catch her around the waist and threaten to spread it all over her face. He wouldn't, though. Instead, he'd lean forward and kiss the whipped cream off her nose.

Whoa. Where had that come from? Did he seriously want to go out with Kelsey again after their last date?

The silence suddenly felt heavy and uncomfortable, and Bryce scrambled for something to say.

"So you're a Batman fan, huh?"

Kelsey nodded, grabbing a bag of grated cheese and placing it in her cart. "Absolutely. He's dark. He's brooding. He's rich. What's not to love?"

Bryce pushed his cart alongside hers, slowing to match her leisurely pace. "You know that Batman's not even a real superhero, right?"

She gasped, stopping in the middle of the aisle to glare at him. "You take that back right now, Bryce Michaels."

He chuckled, shaking his head. "No way. Batman doesn't have any actual powers, just awesome tech."

"The same could be said of Iron Man," Kelsey argued.

"Right. He's also not a superhero."

"You can't be serious!" Kelsey shook her head, grabbing a few cartons of yogurt off the shelf.

He wasn't, but he loved goading her. Loved the playful teasing between them.

"If you don't like Batman or Iron Man, who do you like?" Kelsey demanded.

"I never said I didn't like them—just that they weren't superheroes."

"Okay then. Who's your favorite superhero?"

"Spider-Man," Bryce said confidently.

At that, Kelsey rolled her eyes. "Oh, please. He's an inept high schooler who accidentally got powers. At least Batman has to work for his tech."

They spent the rest of their shopping trip pleasantly arguing over which superheroes were best and why. As they checked out at separate stands and headed toward the parking lot, Bryce couldn't help thinking that this was the best evening he'd had in a long time.

Kelsey paused right outside the sliding glass doors of the store. The sun had set completely now, and the tall floodlights illuminated the mostly empty parking lot. His car sat on one end all alone, and he guessed Kelsey's was near the cluster of cars on the other end.

"Well, I guess I'd better get this stuff home before the ice cream melts," Kelsey said.

"Where are you parked? I'll walk you to your car."

"Oh, I'm okay—"

He fixed her with a stern glare. "I'm not letting you walk to your car alone when it's dark out."

She laughed but didn't argue. He fell into step beside her as she headed toward the more crowded end of the lot. "I go shopping alone after dark all the time. I'm fine, really."

"Maybe so. But I'm also a gentleman."

She paused at a maroon SUV, the headlights flashing as she clicked the key fob. "Well, thanks. I appreciate it."

"No problem."

Bryce helped Kelsey load the few bags into the back of her car, then they stood facing each other, his shopping cart between them.

"I had a lot of fun tonight," Kelsey said finally. "Thanks for keeping me company while we shopped."

"I had fun, too."

She played with her keys, head tilted to the side as she looked up at him. He wanted to ask her if they could hangout sometime. He wanted to ask her out on a date.

But Bryce's courage abandoned him, and he cleared his throat, backing away. "Well, I'd better get this stuff home and put in the fridge. See you later?"

"See you," Kelsey agreed.

Bryce gave a wave and headed toward his car. Why hadn't he asked her out? He was such a coward.

Kelsey waved as she drove by. Bryce waved as well, then quickly loaded up the rest of his groceries and got in his car.

He pulled out his phone, staring at Kelsey's contact info. She wouldn't have given him her number if she didn't want him to text, right? But that had been back when he thought she was Jadyn.

He clicked to send a text and slowly typed one out.

To really determine which superhero is best, we need to come up with some sort of rubric to score them all on.

That didn't sound too stupid, right? They had spent a long time discussing superheroes. Bryce read it over three times, then pushed *send* before he could talk himself out of it.

He immediately regretted his choice. Bryce put the car into gear, muttering, "I am such an idiot." Could he be any lamer?

His phone buzzed as he pulled into the apartment complex. He jerked to a stop, hitting the brakes a little too hard, and quickly checked the text.

It was from Kelsey!

I think you're right. It's the only fair way to determine who is actually the best superhero.

Maybe he wasn't an idiot after all. Bryce texted back with trembling fingers.

After we figure out a way to score them, we'll have to watch all the movies to rate the superheroes.

It was an open-ended invitation—one he really hoped she'd accept. Bryce quickly carried his bags of groceries up to his apartment, stopping three times to check for a reply.

He dumped the bags on his kitchen counter, heart beating rapidly and not from the trip up the flight of stairs.

His phone buzzed, skittering across the counter. He grabbed it, nearly knocking over a gallon of milk in the process.

Oh, I agree completely. We've got to make this happen. The only question is, which movie do we start with?

Bryce's fingers flew across the screen as he texted her back. **Maybe**

**we should get together sometime to figure out this rubric. I want
to make sure you're not skewing things in Batman's favor.**

He waited, heart in his throat, for her reply. When it finally came, he
pumped an enthusiastic fist into the air.

Definitely. Let's pick a date and make this happen.

Chapter Eleven

For the next week, Kelsey devoted most of her work hours to Cheyenne and Zach's wedding. This necessitated two phone calls with Bryce, and each conversation left her nerves tingling at the sound of his husky voice.

But it was the daily texts since their late-night shopping trip that really made her feel all warm and glowy—texts that had nothing to do with Magnolia Gardens. Sometimes they were simple things like *what's your favorite soda?* Other times they were more flirtatious, and usually corny, like *are you a Dalek? Cause you've been rolling through my mind all night.* And sometimes they were deep. Questions like *what do you miss most about Jadyn?*

Their second run-in at the grocery store had just made her like Bryce even more. He'd been teasing and kind, and she'd loved shopping with him.

Why did Jadyn have to have liked Bryce? If she hadn't, he'd be fair game.

He doesn't want you, Kelsey reminded herself. He'd wanted to go out with Jadyn. Kelsey was just a convenient replacement. That was the real issue here. Not her pact with Jadyn.

But Bryce was texting Kelsey, not Jadyn. In fact, the only times he'd brought up her twin in the last week had been when asking Kelsey how she felt about something. The vast majority of their conversations had been about other things. They'd discussed work, of course. But Bryce had also asked Kelsey a hundred questions about herself. He'd flirted outrageously, texting all sorts of nerdy pickup lines. It had been nice.

But every time she giggled over one of those cheesy lines, a little voice whispered that he'd liked Jadyn first. And Kelsey looked exactly like her twin.

On Friday, two weeks after her fateful date with Bryce, Kelsey went with Cheyenne to Magnolia Gardens for a tasting. All of their catering services were on site, which was convenient since Kelsey knew most of her regular caterers would be long booked for August.

When they got to Magnolia Gardens, Bryce was nowhere to be seen. A pretty young girl who barely looked old enough to have graduated high school led them to a small room on the second floor, where a round table was set with a white tablecloth and a short floral arrangement.

"Please have a seat," she said with a smile. "The chef will bring out the appetizer options in just a moment."

"Where's Bryce?" Cheyenne asked, echoing Kelsey's own internal question. They'd texted just last night about their superhero rubric—they'd decided plucky sidekicks should factor into the overall score—and he hadn't said anything about missing this. Since Bryce had been present when they looked at centerpieces a few days ago, she'd assumed he'd be here, too.

"He got called away for a meeting, but he'll be by in about an hour," the young girl said.

The disappointment that flooded over Kelsey was both surprising and unsettling. Why was she being so weird about this? It wasn't like Bryce wasn't coming. And even if he wasn't putting in an appearance, why should Kelsey care? She was the wedding planner, and she and Cheyenne could pick the menu without his input.

Kelsey tried to push Bryce out of her mind as she sat with Cheyenne and offered opinions on the food when asked, but her mind kept straying to him. She was already mentally planning what treats she'd bring when they watched their first superhero movie together. They'd decided that, in the interest of impartiality, they wouldn't watch a Batman or Spider-Man movie first. Maybe they should start with a Marvel film. *Iron Man* was a good place to start.

And that's when Kelsey realized something. She wanted to go out with Bryce again—on a real date, where she was herself and not Jadyn.

Her heart thudded painfully in her chest. Wouldn't going out with Bryce be betraying The Pact? Which, yeah, was kind of silly. It wasn't like Jadyn was around to protest. But Kelsey tenaciously clung to the promise, like honoring it would somehow prove that Jadyn still lived on in some way.

Kelsey tried to focus on the food. She was being ridiculous. High school had been eons ago. Even if Jadyn were still alive, Kelsey doubted she'd care. It wasn't like Jadyn would want to go out with him herself. Not after so many years. Jadyn would probably have been dating some doctor, or attorney, or body builder. She might even have been married by now. There'd been a guy she'd seemed to be growing close to right before her death.

"Sorry I'm late."

Kelsey's mouth grew dry as Bryce breezed into the room. He almost looked dressed down in Dockers and a button-up shirt sans tie, with his shirt sleeves rolled halfway up his forearms. Heat washed over her entire body and she couldn't stop staring.

"We had a new employee orientation for everyone this afternoon," Bryce continued. "It ran longer than I expected."

"Does that mean that we won't see as much of you after today?" Cheyenne asked.

Kelsey held her breath, waiting for the answer.

She should stop spending so much time texting Bryce. Should hope she'd see less of him at work. It wasn't good to let her old crush flare back to life like this.

"You aren't getting rid of me that easily." Bryce's words were directed toward Cheyenne, but his eyes were on Kelsey. Her stomach burned with heat. "I'm seeing this wedding through to the end. The new event coordinator will have to find her own clients."

Cheyenne grinned, and Kelsey's own lips turned up in a smile. She couldn't help it.

"What did I miss?" Bryce asked.

"The lobster bisque, and it's divine," Cheyenne said. "I definitely think that's my choice of soup. I have a feeling that Zach is going to love it, too."

"And where is the groom-to-be?" Bryce asked. His face was open, his interest genuine. Kelsey loved that about him.

Cheyenne heaved a sigh, her eyes sad. "I wish I knew. He's somewhere in the world, doing something for the navy." She made a face. "I hate that he can't tell me more than that. But he assures me nothing will stop him from being at the wedding."

"He's missing out, but I think we've done a pretty good job picking the food without him." Kelsey took a comically loud slurp of lobster bisque, then smacked her lips together in an attempt to make Cheyenne laugh. "Yummy."

"Don't leave me out of the fun." Bryce pulled over a chair and grabbed Kelsey's bowl, sliding it toward him. She watched in fascination as he grabbed her spoon and took a taste. "Wow, this is good."

Kelsey brushed back a strand of hair, unable to stop staring at her spoon in his hand. "Told you so."

He grinned, motioning to the guy in the corner. "The photographer is going to take some pictures while you do the tasting. You know the drill—try to ignore him and act natural."

Cheyenne had no problem doing just that. By the time she had chosen all the food, Kelsey was absolutely stuffed and thoroughly impressed with Magnolia Gardens' catering services. Bryce didn't share her utensils again, but the memory of his lips on her spoon sent shivers of heat up her spine every time she thought of it.

"Sorry I have to rush off," Cheyenne apologized as they rose from the table. "But I should probably be on time for my own bridal shower."

Kelsey laughed, giving her a hug. "I completely understand. Don't worry about the food. Bryce and I will make sure we get it taken care of on this end."

"Thanks. I really appreciate it." Cheyenne grinned. "I can't wait for this wedding."

"Good. You should be excited. It's going to be a perfect day."

But Kelsey wasn't sure she wanted this wedding to ever end. Once it did, what excuse would she have to be near Bryce? Were texts enough to keep their friendship building?

Who else would she talk to about Doctor Who and Harry Potter? Jasmine was great, but she didn't get Kelsey the way Bryce did.

They said goodbye to Cheyenne, then Kelsey followed Bryce down the hallway to his office. She was surprised to see it looked a lot like hers. A minimally cluttered bookcase stood along the back wall. The black desk was mostly empty, with only a few stray pens and post-it notes scattered near the computer. A framed college diploma and tassel hung on one wall.

Bryce sat down behind the desk, motioning to one of the empty chairs in front of it. "It shouldn't take too long for me to get this all entered."

"I'm not in any hurry," Kelsey said, perching on the edge of the chair. She knew it was unnecessary for her to be here while Bryce input the order. He could email her a copy later today, and she could go over it with Cheyenne to make sure everything was right before they approved the menu. But Bryce didn't suggest she leave, and Kelsey didn't bring it up, either.

The click of the keyboard filled the silence between them. Kelsey twisted her hands in her lap, her shoulders aching from the tension there.

Bryce had said he wanted to be friends. Was that really all that the recent texts had been about?

"I'm very impressed with your catering staff," Kelsey said when she couldn't take the quiet anymore. "The food was delicious."

Bryce peeked around the computer monitor, that dimple back in his cheek. "You'll hear no argument from me. I knew Magnolia Gardens needed the best and personally interviewed the executive chefs."

"Must have been a tasty interview," Kelsey joked.

"Oh, it was. I didn't have to make myself dinner for a solid week when we got to second interviews. They all had to prepare a four-course meal for the hiring board to sample."

"Well, you picked a good one," Kelsey said. "Everyone at The Frosted Bride is really excited about this venue. I have a feeling it's going to be a bride favorite in no time."

"I think so, too. This place is so beautiful, it sells itself." He lowered his voice. "Don't tell the owner that, though. He might decide my job isn't as valuable as he thought it was."

Kelsey laughed, nudging his foot under the table with hers. "Don't sell yourself short. Even beautiful, amazing reception centers need a little help from advertising to get noticed."

Bryce leaned across the table, resting his hand gently on top of Kelsey's. Her breathing hitched as she stared into his eyes. There was something in them she couldn't quite figure out, but it made her entire body tremble with anticipation.

"It's been nice working with you these last couple of weeks," Bryce said, his voice husky.

"Yeah, it has. Like Batman and Robin or something. Kelsey and Bryce, saving love one wedding at a time."

Oh gosh. She was so, so lame. Where had that come from?

Bryce ran his thumb over Kelsey's knuckles, his touch so light she wondered if she'd imagined it. "You're definitely Batman in that scenario. It's obvious that you're really good at your job, and I can tell Cheyenne adores you."

Kelsey abruptly pulled her hand away. Bryce had adored someone else once, too. But it hadn't been Kelsey.

She brushed a strand of hair behind one ear, trying to act casual. "I try to give all my brides a positive experience. A wedding should be magical, not stressful."

"Not only are you beautiful, you're wise, too."

Her cheeks burned with heat. Kelsey gave a nervous chuckle and rose to her feet. She had to get out of here. Had to take a step back and clear her head. "Seems like you've got this under control. Think you can finish up on your own?"

Bryce's face fell as he rose, too. The sparkle disappeared from his eyes as he gave a hesitant nod. "Uh, yeah. Sure."

"Great. Call me if you have any questions." She hurried from the room before he could protest.

What was wrong with her? All she'd thought about for days was Bryce. And here she was, running away like a coward. He'd been sending her all the right signals. Kelsey was just too afraid to make a move.

Why did he have to like Jadyn? Kelsey heaved a sigh as she pushed through the front doors of Magnolia Gardens. Yes, Jadyn might be dead. Bryce had forever missed his chance with that Wilkes twin. But that didn't mean he couldn't like Kelsey for herself. The things they had in common were all things Jadyn hadn't liked.

If only Jadyn would give her some sort of a sign that it was okay to make a move and ask Bryce out. A reassurance that his motives were pure or whatever. Angels surely had access to that sort of information. No doubt Jadyn was content dating some sexy pirate in heaven. Kelsey knew that Jadyn wouldn't hold her to The Pact—not if Bryce really was a guy worth dating.

She strode quickly across the parking lot, heat radiating up from the blacktop and making her entire body uncomfortably warm. How was she supposed to face Bryce the next time they saw each other? Maybe she'd text him later tonight and apologize for running out so fast. Claim she'd had a headache or something.

"Kelsey, wait!"

Bryce sprinted across the parking lot. Kelsey's heart began to hammer, and she put a hand to her neck, biting her bottom lip.

"Did you forget something?" she asked.

Bryce shook his head, his breathing heavy. "No. You ran out of there so fast that it took me by surprise. Is everything okay?"

"Of course." Kelsey forced a smile, hoping it didn't tremble as much as her knees. Had he really just chased after her?

"Oh." Bryce scratched the back of his neck, seeming to deflate. "That's good. I thought you seemed upset back there or something, but maybe I was imagining things."

"Just a long day. I guess I'm tired or something."

The question was on the tip of her tongue, begging for release. She wanted so badly to ask him outright if he liked her for herself, and not for her connection to Jadyn.

But she was a coward and instead stared at her shoes.

A hand softly grasped hers, sending her senses into overdrive. Bryce's eyes were soft, his brow furrowed in concern. "You can tell me anything, Kelsey. I'm here if you need to talk."

Kelsey closed her eyes, holding back tears. She couldn't do this. If it turned out that Bryce was using her as a replacement for Jadyn, she'd be crushed.

"Hey." His voice was soft and husky as he squeezed her hand in reassurance. "I don't want to pry, but I do want to help."

"You wouldn't understand." Her voice sounded strangled.

"Maybe not. But I'd like to." If possible, his voice dipped even lower. His eyes darkened with an emotion that made her insides quiver. "I really like you, Kelsey. I've loved getting to know you these past two weeks, and I'd really like to take you on a date. That is, if you'll let me."

Her breath caught.

"A *real* date," Bryce clarified. His mouth quirked up in a grin, and the dimple made its appearance. "One where you're Kelsey and I'm Bryce, and we aren't super awkward and uncomfortable the whole time."

Kelsey wanted that, too. Bryce certainly seemed genuine, and her sixteen-year-old self was already screaming at her for not immediately accepting the offer.

She sent up a silent plea to Jadyn—*tell me if I'm about to make a mistake!*

Bryce's hand caressed her cheek, brushing back a strand of hair that had been caught by the wind. Kelsey tilted her chin up so that she could look into his eyes.

She wanted this. So why shouldn't she go out with him? They were both single. He seemed interested. She definitely was.

But fear still lodged itself in her throat, preventing a *yes* from slipping past.

Help me! she silently pleaded to Jadyn, wherever she was.

And that's when Kelsey saw it. A red balloon floated lazily toward the clouds, a cheerful drop against the darkening night sky. Her fingers flew to the tattoo behind her ear as she sucked in a breath.

The wind caught the balloon, driving it closer toward Kelsey. She could almost hear Jadyn's reassurances on the breeze—*It's okay. Bryce likes you, Kels. Go out with him. I'm doing just fine here in heaven.*

"Kelsey?"

She tore her gaze away from the balloon and focused on Bryce. "Sorry," she breathed.

"I hope I'm not being too forward." Bryce shifted, rubbing the back of his neck. "I know we kind of got off to a rocky start, but I thought we'd been getting along pretty well these last few weeks. I know I've really enjoyed our texts, but if all you want is friendship, I understand. It's okay if you don't want to go out with me."

"That's not it at all." Kelsey captured his hand, loving the way he instantly curled his fingers around hers in a protective cocoon.

She couldn't believe her high school fantasy was finally coming true. But the ten-year wait only made this moment that much sweeter.

"I'd love to go out with you, Bryce Michaels. Name the day and I'll be there."

Chapter Twelve

Kelsey glanced at Bryce, her heart fluttering. He seemed to sense her gaze and looked over with a grin. That dimple was going to be her undoing today. If she made it through the date without kissing it, then immediately regretting the action, she'd consider it a miracle.

She couldn't believe she was on a date with Bryce—as herself and not as Jadyn. They'd texted almost constantly in the days leading up to the date, but he hadn't given her much information about today's plans. When she'd asked, he'd said to dress casually and plan for a day spent outdoors.

"Aren't you going to tell me where we're going?" Kelsey asked. They were on the freeway, but headed out of the city and toward the mountains that surrounded Los Angeles.

"I like keeping our destination a secret," Bryce teased. "You're cute when you're anxious."

She blushed. "Seriously, where are we going?"

He just shook his head. "Not telling. But you're going to love it. Promise."

Kelsey was pretty sure that Bryce could take her to a mortuary for a tour and she'd be thrilled. She was so gone on him it wasn't even funny. "If you say so."

They turned off the freeway and began climbing along the canyon road. Buildings gave way to leafy trees with an occasional waterfall cascading off the mountain. Kelsey began to recognize the road as they wound their way toward a popular resort.

"Hiking?" she asked. It was supposed to be a beautiful late-spring day. Kelsey wasn't the most coordinated of hikers, but she did just fine on easy trails. Hopefully there wouldn't be steep, rocky paths to trip and embarrass herself on.

Bryce shook his head. He'd been smiling nonstop since picking her up, and Kelsey couldn't help thinking that had to be a good sign. "Nope."

"Mountain biking?" she tried again. That would be even worse for her coordination, but it sounded fun, too. Jadyn had always been athletic, and Kelsey had learned to enjoy outdoor activities by default.

Again, Bryce shook his head. "Seriously, you'll never guess. I've always wanted to do this, but I've never gotten around to it."

Kelsey furrowed her brow, completely stumped. The resort was a popular spot for outdoor concerts, but those usually happened at night. She'd never been to the resort and wasn't really sure what else there was to do there.

Bryce pulled into the parking lot and Kelsey got out of the car, gasping at the view. The Swiss-style chalet sat against the backdrop of a lush green mountainside. Latticed eaves framed the gables. Purple wildflowers added pops of color on the hillside.

"It looks like a gingerbread house!" she said.

"You've never been here?"

"No. I guess that means it'll be the first visit for both of us."

"I think I like the sound of that." Bryce pulled a baseball cap onto his head, then settled one onto Kelsey's. "I brought sunscreen, too, but figured this would help you not get sunburned today."

His thoughtfulness made her feel as though her heart had been filled with helium—light and airy.

Happy.

Wow. She hadn't been this happy since before Jadyn's death. How had she not seen that before now? And it was all because of Bryce.

She batted her eyes, placing a hand on one hip as she struck a pose. "How do I look?"

Bryce grinned, tapping her nose with a finger. "Absolutely adorable."

Kelsey pulled off the blue hat, noting the gold logo for the Los Angeles Coyotes. The hat was almost identical to Bryce's. "I didn't realize you were a football fan."

The tips of his ears glowed red. "I'm not really. But when I stopped in the store last night, the cashier told me girls are crazy about Wyatt James and they can barely keep Coyote hats in stock. So I figured it was a safe bet you'd be happy to wear it."

He'd bought the hats just for today. Her heart was definitely filled with helium, because right now she was walking on Cloud Nine. "I will gladly wear this hat all day. And not because it's Wyatt James's team."

"Does that mean you'll let me hold your hand right now?"

"I'm a pretty klutzy person, and this parking lot is covered in gravel."

"Well then, I'd better help you." Bryce took her hand gently in his, and that's when Kelsey knew that today was going to be perfect.

They crossed the parking lot and followed a paved walkway that led away from the resort. Tall grasses and scrub brush lined the side of the walkway, which meandered toward a line of trees in the distance.

"Are you going to tell me where we're going now?" Kelsey asked.

Bryce pointed to the trees that looked like miniatures, they were so far away. "We're doing that."

Kelsey squinted and realized the trees climbed up a hill, which was dotted with people. A long, white line went right through the middle of the trees. "Is that a track?"

"Yeah. You ride down it on carts. It's called the Alpine Slide."

A faint squeal pierced the air as someone in the distance flew down the mountainside. Kelsey laughed, clutching Bryce's hand tighter. "I've heard of this."

"Are you excited?"

His face was so hopeful. She wasn't about to let him down.

Kelsey squeezed his hand, nodding enthusiastically. "Absolutely. It looks like a lot of fun. One of my brides came here for her bachelorette party, and the bridesmaids were all talking about it at the wedding."

"I'm glad you like it. I was hoping you would."

Kelsey was certain she would love anything Bryce planned, because he always did things thoughtfully.

Bryce paid for all-day passes, then they waited in a short line and boarded the ski lift that would take them to the top. He rested his arm on the back of the bench and Kelsey snuggled close, staring in awe as they rose over the treetops. An unusually rainy spring had the mountainside bursting with green growth.

"You aren't afraid of heights, are you?" Bryce asked.

"Not at all." Kelsey gasped, pointing to a family of deer as they pranced down the mountain. "This is amazing!"

"Look, there's a raccoon."

Kelsey laughed. "I love it. So I take it you aren't afraid of heights, either?"

"Not when I'm safely in a ski lift." His voice softened as his hand rested on her shoulder, pulling her more tightly against him. "Not when I'm with you."

The ride up the mountainside was over much too quickly. At the top, they waited in another line for the slide. Kelsey listened to the squeals and screams of those who went before them, her anticipation mounting with each exclamation.

Eventually it was their turn. Bryce helped Kelsey into the cart, which kind of looked like snow sleds she'd seen in movies. As he sat behind her, Kelsey was acutely aware of where his legs touched along the length of hers. Bryce's arms came tightly around her waist, gripping the brake that was between their legs. She leaned back into him, her entire body sizzling with heat.

The hill suddenly seemed a lot longer, and a lot steeper. The people at the bottom were mere pinpricks, and her stomach did a somersault as she considered the steep decline.

"Ready?" Bryce whispered in her ear.

Kelsey wrapped her arms around his, securing them together. She took a deep breath. "Ready."

Bryce pulled up on the cart's brake and they careened down the track. Kelsey let out a squeal as warm air rushed past her face and the trees went by in a blur. Bryce's arms tightened around her waist as she leaned into him.

Kelsey laughed, feeling freer than she ever had before. Her stomach gave a happy roll as they bounced over one of the dips in the track. The slide screeched against the track, sending a flock of birds scattering from a nearby tree.

"Having fun?" Bryce asked, his lips pressed against her ear so she could hear him.

"Yes!" Kelsey laughed. "You?"

"Definitely."

The end of the track loomed ahead. Kelsey's fingernails dug into Bryce's arm as it approached at a frightening speed. It was coming much too quickly.

They were going to crash.

Kelsey closed her eyes, biting back a scream. She held tighter to Bryce, turning her face into his arm.

The cart came to a sudden halt, the force jerking her and Bryce forward. But they were still firmly in the cart.

Kelsey opened one eye, then the other. A toddler stared at her from behind the railing, two fingers in his mouth and a red balloon tied to one arm. A mere foot of track was left in front of Bryce and Kelsey.

She sagged back against Bryce, her limbs suddenly limp. "I thought we were going to crash."

"'Random chance seems to have operated in our favor,'" Bryce quoted.

"Star Trek." She turned around, nudging him in the shoulder.

He grinned, and that darn dimple would've buckled her knees had she been standing. "Of course. And for the record, I knew we weren't going to crash."

"Sure you did."

Bryce jumped out of the cart and held out a hand to Kelsey. "Want to go again?"

"Absolutely." Kelsey let him pull her out of the cart, happy when he didn't let go. They headed back toward the ski lift, still hand-in-hand.

"Does that mean you liked it?" Bryce asked.

"I loved it. Near-death experience and all."

"Please. We were totally safe."

Kelsey snorted, giving an exaggerated eye roll. "Admit it. You were scared, too."

"I was cool as a cucumber the entire time."

"On your left!" someone called from behind.

Kelsey glanced over her shoulder and saw a bicyclist speeding toward them. Bryce grabbed her around the waist, pulling her off the path.

She stumbled, hands flat against Bryce's chest and knocking them both off balance. He grunted, tightening his hold around her waist as his knees hit the back of a bench she hadn't even realized was there. She let out a little yelp as she was pulled down onto the bench with Bryce.

Right onto his lap.

"Sorry!" Kelsey scrambled to move away from him, but Bryce tightened his hold with a chuckle.

"Where are you going?" he asked.

"To chase after the bicyclist, I guess." Her voice sounded embarrassingly breathy. "He should apologize for tripping us or something."

"I don't mind."

She was suddenly all too aware that his face was mere inches away. Her hand was resting on his chest, and he placed his hand over hers, holding it in place. The air was suddenly filled with an electricity she didn't want to shake.

Bryce reached up, tugging her baseball cap back into place. She hadn't even realized it had been knocked loose in the fall.

"You're so beautiful," Bryce whispered.

She bit her lip, looking down at where his hand covered hers.

"Who do you see when you look at me?" she asked in a whisper. "Kelsey? Or Jadyn?"

If he said Jadyn, she would die. Today had been everything to her.

"Only Kelsey."

Her eyes flew up to meet Bryce's. There was no deceit there. No hint of trying to spare her feelings. Only complete and total honesty.

"Really?"

"Really," he agreed.

Bryce wrapped a hand around the back of her neck, and her heart actually stopped beating for a moment.

He was going to kiss her. She knew it. Kelsey let her eyes flutter shut and mouth part.

His lips landed on her cheek in the softest of touches. Her eyes flew open, but she saw only desire in his. Disappointment was quickly drowned out by excitement.

This was only their first date. There'd be plenty of time for kissing later.

"Come on," Bryce said quietly. "Let's go down the hill again."

They spent the next two hours flying down the mountainside, and Kelsey loved every moment of it. When their faces were flushed with heat and shirts sticky with perspiration, they trudged back to the lodge and cooled down over frozen lemonades while debating the merits of their favorite fandoms.

Kelsey had never enjoyed herself so much on a date. The glimmer in Bryce's eyes told her that he was having just as much fun as she was.

Hours later, she held his hand as they slowly walked up the steps to her apartment. Kelsey leaned against her door, wanting to draw this out as long as possible.

"I had a great time today. Thanks for taking me to the resort."

Bryce brushed her hair behind one ear, tipping her baseball cap up. He'd left his in the car, but told her to keep hers. "I had a great time today, too. I don't remember the last time I had this much fun."

Kelsey stared into his blue eyes, breathless. "Me either."

Bryce leaned toward her, their faces mere inches apart. "I hope we can have fun again soon."

"I wouldn't be opposed to that." Kelsey took a hold of his arms to steady herself, unwittingly drawing herself closer to him.

That was all the encouragement Bryce needed. His hands threaded in her hair, knocking the baseball cap loose. Then his lips were brushing against hers.

Kelsey wrapped her arms around his neck, pressing herself closer. His lips were warm and full, and somehow both soft and firm. She yanked her hat off, not wanting anything to get in the way of this moment. Bryce's hands pressed against the small of her back, urging her closer as he deepened the kiss.

This was what heaven felt like. Her sixteen-year-old fantasies hadn't even come close to a real life kiss with Bryce Michaels.

His lips moved against hers while Kelsey's heart soared. She'd never been kissed like this before.

"Jadyn," Bryce whispered, his breath bathing her face.

Kelsey froze, the heady euphoria she'd felt mere moments ago instantly evaporating. She put her hands on his chest and pushed him back. His eyes were clouded with emotion and his brow wrinkled in confusion.

"What did you call me?" Kelsey demanded.

She saw the moment he realized his mistake. All the desire vanished from his eyes as they widened in horror.

"Kelsey," he said quickly. "I meant to call you Kelsey."

"But that isn't what you said. You called me Jadyn." Kelsey held a trembling hand to her lips, leaning against the door for support.

He'd been using her as nothing more than a stand-in.

"It was an accident." Bryce placed a hand on the door near her head, his expression pleading. "Kelsey, I'm so sorry. I swear, it was an honest mistake. Please—"

"A mistake?" She pushed his hand away, fumbling for the key.

"I didn't mean anything by it. We've had such a great day. I don't want to leave it like this."

She laughed incredulously, shaking her head. Her hands trembled, and it took two tries to properly insert the key into the lock. She twisted the knob and threw the door open.

"Kels—"

She whirled, glaring up at the face that moments ago had made her heart flutter with happiness. Tears burned, but she wasn't about to let him see them.

"Don't call or text me," Kelsey said. Then she slammed the door in his face.

A fist immediately pounded on the door. "I'm so, so sorry. Please. Open up the door and let's talk."

Kelsey put a hand to her mouth, tears spilling down her cheeks.

"Give me another chance. Please, Kels." His voice broke on the last word.

That had been the best kiss she'd ever experienced in her life. And he'd only been kissing her because she looked like Jadyn.

Kelsey leaned against the door and slid to the floor, her shoulders shaking with silent sobs.

Bryce didn't try to talk to her again.

Chapter Thirteen

Bryce pounded a fist against Kelsey's closed apartment door, feeling sick.

He couldn't believe he'd said Jadyn's name. Why had he done that?

"I'm so, so sorry," Bryce said, his voice thick with emotion. "Please. Open up the door and let's talk."

He pressed his ear against the door, straining to hear something. Praying she'd fling the door open, even if it sent him tumbling to the floor in a heap.

Nothing.

"Give me another chance." He rested a trembling hand against the door, panic clawing at his throat. The early summer heat suddenly felt oppressive. He could feel his shirt sticking uncomfortably to his skin. Felt like he was inhaling water. "Please, Kels."

No response. She wasn't opening that door. Wouldn't talk to him again, at least not tonight.

Bryce closed his eyes as bile burned his throat, the acid choking him. He'd finally met a girl he could see himself falling in love with. No, that wasn't quite accurate.

He was falling in love with Kelsey. And he'd totally blown it.

Bryce took a deep breath. The hurt in her eyes when he'd said her sister's name had sliced through the hazy cloud of desire and brought him crashing back to earth. She had every right to be furious about his behavior. He owed it to her to give her space tonight, if that's what she wanted.

He ran his fingers lightly over the door, wishing Kelsey would open it up so he could explain. But she didn't, so instead he walked away.

How had Jadyn's name popped out of his mouth?

He shoved his hands deep in his pockets, walking slowly toward his car. He'd been kissing Kelsey and enjoying every moment of it. Kelsey, the girl he'd had a serious crush on for an entire term in tenth grade.

Bryce's mind had wandered back to high school as their kiss deepened. He'd been thinking about how incredibly grateful he was that he'd never asked Jadyn out. If he had, it would have ruined any chance he had in the here and now with Kelsey. That was unthinkable.

He'd put his hand behind Kelsey's neck, urging her closer. Tilting her head for better access to her mouth. And the thought had come to him, unbidden—he was glad that, if the universe had decreed that one of the Wilkes twins must die, it hadn't been Kelsey.

The traitorous thought in the midst of the most amazing kiss of his life had instantly slammed Bryce with guilt. He'd deepened the kiss, trying to wipe the awful thought from his mind.

And somehow, in the midst of his turmoil, Jadyn's name had popped out. His never quiet mind had ultimately put the nail in his own coffin.

Bryce put his car into gear, chuckling darkly. Coffin. Talk about morbid, considering where Jadyn was.

It took every ounce of willpower he possessed to drive away from Kelsey's apartment. His mind screamed for him to pound on her door and demand they talk about this. Insist she let him explain. But he wasn't that type of guy, and he'd respect her wishes and leave. At least for tonight.

He had to fix this. If he could just find the perfect way to apologize to Kelsey, maybe she would forgive him. Maybe she'd give him a second chance.

But how could he apologize for something so awful?

He was still trying to come up with a way to express to Kelsey just how sorry he was when he arrived at Magnolia Gardens the next day. They had their first event tonight, a quinceañera. Bryce needed to be on his A game, but he couldn't get the look of betrayal on Kelsey's face out of his mind.

He couldn't blame her for feeling betrayed by his word. Bryce felt sick every time he thought of what he'd done to Kelsey. How badly he'd hurt her.

Bryce had thought of Kelsey the entire time they were kissing. Had been over-the-moon happy that she was the one he was with. But why would she believe him after what he'd said? If the situation was reversed, he'd definitely have some doubts.

In his office, Bryce pulled up his task list for the day, trying to focus. Right now, he didn't know how to fix things with Kelsey. But he did know how to make sure tonight's event was spectacular, and he needed to focus on that. This first party at Magnolia Gardens was crucial and could make or break their reputation going forward. It needed to be perfect. After tonight, he'd have two entire days off work to figure out how to fix things with Kelsey.

A soft knock sounded at the office door. Bryce looked up, surprised to see Cheyenne standing there with Zach right behind her.

He rose quickly. Had he forgotten an appointment? Unlikely, because that would mean forgetting about an opportunity to spend time with Kelsey. This must be an unscheduled visit.

"Zach. Cheyenne. What can I do for you?"

"We got a call this morning asking us to drop by and sign a photograph release form or something?" Cheyenne lifted her shoulder in a shrug, her large cream-color bag rising with the motion. "It was a woman who left the message. She said we must have missed that form when signing the contracts."

"I haven't heard anything about that, but let me check my email." Bryce sat back down, feeling flustered. He didn't like being caught off guard.

Kelsey probably didn't, either. And she must feel like she'd been hit with a truck after last night.

Bryce took a deep breath, trying to clear his head. He quickly found the email, which had been sent yesterday evening—about the same time he was ruining everything with Kelsey.

"Found it," Bryce said, opening the release form. "I am so sorry about this you guys. Let me print it off so you guys can be on your way."

"No worries. We're not in a rush or anything." Cheyenne gazed up at Zach, her eyes glowing with love. Would Kelsey ever look at Bryce like that?

The printer whirred as it started up. Bryce tapped his desk impatiently, offering what he hoped was an apologetic smile. "I hope you didn't make a special trip out here just for this. It isn't so urgent that it couldn't wait until you were here next time. I'll make sure to talk to the secretary about it." He mentally added talking to the secretary to his task list. Obviously she needed a refresher on which forms needed to be signed immediately and which could wait. Not a big deal, but he felt bad Cheyenne and Zach had taken time out of their day just for this.

"It's fine, really." Cheyenne grasped Zach's hand, smiling up at him. "We were already headed this way and figured we'd drop in and get it taken care of. Things have been so crazy lately with the wedding, so we decided to take a day off from planning things and just have fun."

"Well then, I'll get you on your way as quickly as possible," Bryce said. He glanced at the printer—it was nearly done.

Zach grinned, leaning down to kiss Cheyenne on the cheek. "As long as I'm with Cheyenne, I don't care what we're doing."

The printer grew silent, and Bryce grabbed the paper off the tray. It warmed his hands and left the faint smell of toner in the office. He slid it across the table to them, along with a pen. "Still, I'm sure you'd rather spend the day somewhere else. You can take a minute to read the form if you'd like, but all it says is that Magnolia Gardens has permission to use any of the videos or photographs we've taken as we see fit in marketing campaigns."

"We trust you." Cheyenne signed with a flourish, handing the pen over to Zach. "We do want to get going before it gets too hot out. Zach's taking me to the boardwalk, just like on our first date."

Zach wasn't quite as hasty as Cheyenne and picked up the form, scanning through it.

Bryce leaned back in his chair, in no rush. "Must have been a good first date."

Cheyenne leaned her head on Zach's shoulder, eyes sparkling. "Good enough I went out with him a second time."

"Thank heavens for that." Zach signed the paper as well, apparently satisfied with what it said.

"It wasn't the date that made me say yes so much as how well Zach knew me," Cheyenne said. "I knew he liked the person I was. Zach knows me better than anyone in this world, and he still loves me."

"That I do." Zach kissed Cheyenne on the forehead, rising. "Is that all you needed from us, Bryce?"

"Yes. Sorry again about the mix-up, and thanks for coming down."

"Not a problem." Zach reached a hand across the desk, giving Bryce's a firm shake. "Have a good day."

Bryce said goodbye to both of them, then sat back in his chair. Cheyenne's words had sparked an idea.

He knew how to get his second chance with Kelsey. He had to prove to her that he knew who she truly was, and that's why he liked her. That it was Kelsey he was falling in love with, not Jadyn.

He had to get to work.

Chapter Fourteen

Kelsey wasn't sure how long she sat on the floor and cried before finally calling Jasmine. Before she could finish blubbering out the whole horrible story, Jasmine was at her door with a carton of ice cream.

She'd never been so grateful for her friend.

Kelsey spent the night crying while Jasmine called Bryce nasty names and tried her best to make Kelsey feel better. She ate an entire pint of ice cream, but all it accomplished was giving her a stomachache.

Jadyn. She couldn't believe he had called her that, especially in the middle of a kiss. Kelsey's heart twisted every time she remembered that moment—the moment he'd crushed her heart.

She'd almost believed that Bryce liked her, maybe even in an I-have-a-crush-on-you sort of way. He'd asked her out, hadn't he? But he'd been pining for Jadyn all along.

When the ice cream was gone and Kelsey's tears were spent, Jasmine left with promises to check on Kelsey tomorrow. So Kelsey changed into her pajamas and crawled into bed. She curled around a pillow, her eyes dry and gritty from crying.

It had been impossibly hard to lose Jadyn. Kelsey had wanted to die herself at first. How was she supposed to go on as one half of a whole?

But that loss had only been compounded by the pain on her friends' and family's faces every time they looked at Kelsey. She was a physical reminder of what they'd lost.

Gradually, Kelsey had distanced herself from everyone she'd been close to before the accident. Not even her parents had protested the emotional distance. She only saw them once a month for dinner now, and the evenings were always uncomfortable affairs that left her crying on the drive home.

And she knew everyone loved her, especially her parents. But they loved Jadyn, too. It was part of why Kelsey valued her friendship with Jasmine so much now. She'd only ever known Kelsey as herself, not as part of a duo. When everyone else looked at Kelsey, they saw both twins.

But apparently Bryce only saw one of them. Jadyn.

Kelsey didn't leave the house the next day. Instead, she watched reruns of her favorite TV shows—nothing romantic or superhero themed, since that would only remind her of Bryce—and ate a bowl of cookie dough. After another long night that included very little rest, Kelsey finally rolled out of bed at six a.m.

If she couldn't sleep, she might as well go for a walk and try to clear her head. Her throat ached and head pounded from last night's emotions. There was a donut shop only a block away from her apartment. She'd bury her sorrows in glazed donuts.

Kelsey opened her front door and tripped. She threw out her arms, catching herself before falling. What in the world?

She frowned, staring at the six-pack of Dr. Pepper that was on the welcome mat. A note was taped to the top of it, the chicken scratch handwriting a faint shadow against the white paper.

Kelsey glanced up and down the breezeway. The wind was already hot and humid today, and leaves rustled on the nearby trees. But she saw no sign of whoever had left this strange gift.

She bent down, carefully peeling the note from the cans. Kelsey squinted, trying to make out the unfamiliar handwriting.

THE LEANING TOWER of Pisa is considered one of history's greatest mistakes. It took one hundred and seventy-seven years to build, then started leaning only ten years after it was finished. But now it's a huge tourist attraction. Millions of people a year travel from all around the world to admire the structure. Maybe that means not all mistakes have to turn out bad.

KELSEY CRUMPLED up the note in disgust. Was this Bryce's idea of an apology? No way was she going to let him minimize what he'd done by comparing his mistake to a famous architectural landmark.

She glared at the soda and headed down the stairs, anger making each step pound. By the time she hit the street corner, she was running. It had been one of Jadyn's favorite hobbies, and Kelsey had usually been coerced into joining her. But she hadn't run since the memorial service.

What a jerk. Like soda could make up for what Bryce had done. She blew past the donut shop, her stomach churning. No way she could eat anything now.

He'd kissed her. Looked into her eyes. Caressed her face.

Made her feel like the only woman in the world.

And then he'd called her by her twin sister's name. The sister he'd admitted to having a crush on. The sister that had left a gaping hole in Kelsey's chest—one she knew would never fully heal.

Except that Kelsey had pretended to be Jadyn just to get a date with Bryce. He'd forgiven her for that without qualification. Even in the middle of confessing her lies, Bryce had been nothing but gracious and kind.

By the time she passed by the donut shop on her return trip, Kelsey's anger had simmered down. She stopped inside and bought a dozen glazed donuts, her thoughts churning. Was she being unfair to Bryce by not forgiving him?

Probably.

Kelsey chomped through a donut as she slowly walked home, trying to take her emotions out of the equation. It wasn't like Bryce had intentionally called her Jadyn. He might not even have realized he was using Kelsey as her sister's replacement.

She could forgive him, Kelsey decided. Not today, but eventually. But that didn't mean she was going to date him.

Back at the apartment, the soda still waited for her in the exact same spot. She gave it a glare and opened the apartment door, then paused. It wasn't the soda's fault Bryce was a jerk.

In the spirit of forgiveness, she carefully picked up the Dr. Pepper and went inside, pulling a can from the ring.

Jasmine texted a few hours later, and they decided to go grocery shopping together. Kelsey was running dangerously low on a few essentials, like ice cream and the ingredients for brownies. Kelsey volunteered to drive, and they agreed to meet in the parking lot in five minutes. Would it be weird if she suggested they shop at a different store than their usual? That grocery store held so many memories of Bryce.

She was still a few car lengths away when she saw a small cooler sitting on the hood of her SUV.

Kelsey strode forward and yanked the lid off. A giant chocolate bar —her favorite brand—was nestled among the freezer packs keeping it cool. She turned the lid over, searching for the note she knew would be there, and snatched it up.

COLUMBUS MISTAKENLY DISCOVERED America when he was trying to find India. Instead of finding a new trade route, he introduced an array of new foods to the European diet—foods like chocolate. Maybe it wasn't such a mistake after all?

"HE ALSO INTRODUCED smallpox to the Native Americans," Kelsey muttered.

"Who gave people smallpox?" Jasmine asked.

Kelsey quickly put the lid back on the cooler. Jasmine stared at her, one dark eyebrow raised in question. She'd pulled back her inky black hair into a high ponytail, and her dark skin had only the lightest dusting of makeup.

"Bryce thinks he's being clever or something." Kelsey handed the note to Jasmine and motioned to the cooler. "There was a pack of my favorite soda on the porch with another note this morning."

Jasmine read the note, then grinned, handing it back. She peeked into the cooler and her grin widened. "Wow, he must feel really bad about what he did. Dr. Pepper and chocolate? He knows you pretty well."

"Yeah, well, Bryce and I have known each other for a long time." Although now that she thought about it, he'd probably only learned those two things about her more recently. It wasn't like they'd spent much time hanging out in high school, and she hadn't been a soda drinker until college.

"I bet he doesn't know any of this stuff about Jadyn," Jasmine said.

Kelsey frowned, not liking the way her heart fluttered at that thin strand of hope. "Are we going to sit here all day and talk about my disastrous love life, or are we going to go grocery shopping before the Saturday crowds hit?"

"Sorry." Jasmine held up her hands in surrender as Kelsey unlocked the door and tossed the cooler of chocolate on the back seat. "You don't want to talk about it. I can respect that."

Now Kelsey felt bad. She shouldn't have snapped at Jasmine. "No, I'm sorry. This whole thing just has me on edge."

Jasmine pantomimed zipping her lips. "Did you watch this week's episode of *Eye in the Sky* yet? That head honcho competition was nuts."

Over the course of that day and the next, Kelsey found four more gifts from Bryce. There was a gift card to her favorite ice cream parlor with a Thomas Edison quote on failure. A Batman key chain with a reminder that penicillin was accidentally discovered by Sir Andrew Fleming. Tickets to a movie theater with a short history lesson on how chocolate chip cookies were created after Ruth Wakefield ran out of baking chocolate and tried to substitute semi-sweet.

The last package arrived the following evening, three days after their fateful kiss. Kelsey opened the door to find Jasmine holding it, a sympathetic smile on her lips.

"Are you kidding me?" Kelsey asked, taking the small wrapped package. "This is getting ridiculous. Can't he take a hint?"

"It was on the doorstep when I got here," Jasmine said.

"I have no idea how he's delivering them so secretly."

"Maybe he's a ninja." Jasmine leaned forward, her chin in her hand. "*Eye in the Sky* can wait. What is it?"

Kelsey yanked off the wrapping paper with a growl. But all of her anger vanished when she saw the framed picture from their date on the Alpine Slide. She gently ran a finger over their faces. They both looked so happy in that photo. So alive.

She tugged the note from one corner of the frame. Had she misjudged Bryce?

CALLING *my (hopefully future) girlfriend by her sister's name is a pretty big mistake. But I think it's one we can recover from, if you'll give me a second chance. I may have said Jadyn, but all I was thinking about was Kelsey. That's a promise. Please, Kels. Let me make this up to you. I'm so, so sorry.*

"HE SEEMS PRETTY SINCERE."

Kelsey jumped, clasping the note to her chest. Jasmine grinned, not looking the least bit ashamed that she'd been reading over Kelsey's shoulder.

"Give him another chance," Jasmine encouraged. "I really think it might have been an honest mistake on his part. You do look like Jadyn, and that's the girl he's been crushing on for a decade. He can't be the first person to call you by her name. I'm sure your parents mixed you up all the time."

"Yeah, when they were telling us to pick up our socks or do our homework." Kelsey blinked back tears. "But Bryce and I were kissing. That was the best kiss of my life, and he said Jadyn. Don't you think that means something? He's using me as her replacement."

"Maybe. Maybe not." Jasmine shrugged. "Either way, I think it's worth giving him another shot. I've never seen you like this over a guy, and he's trying so hard to apologize."

"No." Kelsey shook her head, brushing back tears. "It hurts too much."

"Probably about as much as finding out he was on a date with the wrong twin."

Kelsey pointed the note at Jasmine with a trembling hand. "That's a low blow."

"It's also the truth. He forgave you for pretending to be Jadyn. Don't you think you should forgive him for calling you by her name?"

"I don't want to talk about this anymore," Kelsey said roughly. "Drop it."

But Kelsey couldn't help wondering if Jasmine was right.

Chapter Fifteen

Kelsey woke up the next morning with the awful realization that she'd have to see Bryce today. Cheyenne and Zach had an appointment at Magnolia Gardens to finalize the table centerpieces.

As Kelsey got ready for work, she prayed with everything she was worth that Bryce wouldn't be at the meeting. He'd said the new employees started today. Maybe, given their disastrous second date, he'd let the event coordinator take over.

But Bryce had said he would see this wedding through to the end, no matter what. She had a feeling he wouldn't pass up the chance to corner her.

When Kelsey arrived with Cheyenne and Zach, Bryce was waiting for them in the showroom. His eyes locked onto Kelsey's, apologetic and full of regret. For a brief moment in time, everyone else disappeared. It was just Bryce and Kelsey, and they were having a fantastic time on the Alpine Slide, and she knew he'd kiss her before the date was over.

She swallowed hard, reminding herself that he had kissed her—and broken her heart.

Today, Kelsey would accept his apology. She'd even try to be gracious about it. But that was it. The Pop Rocks in her stomach would have to find someone else to jump for joy over.

She was no one's stand-in. Not even Jadyn's.

Kelsey tried to remain present while Cheyenne debated various centerpiece options. Zach was the perfect groom, offering his opinion when asked but easily going along with whatever Cheyenne leaned toward. But as Kelsey complimented Cheyenne on her vision and offered suggestions when asked, she was aware of Bryce's hot gaze on her.

He wasn't going to let her disappear without talking about that kiss. Kelsey swallowed hard, nodding as Cheyenne pointed to a tall vase of calla lilies. It was a good thing Cheyenne had a keen eye for design, because Kelsey was no help.

This meeting was lasting an eternity, and Kelsey feared she might spontaneously ignite before it was through.

At long last, Cheyenne made her final selections with Zach's support.

"I think those will look beautiful," Bryce said as he finished filling out the order form. "You have great taste."

"Thanks." Cheyenne beamed, turning to Kelsey. "You can finish this up, right? Zach's best man just got into town, and we're meeting him for dinner."

Bryce folded his arms, watching Kelsey with an unreadable expression. She swallowed hard, focusing on Cheyenne. "Absolutely. Have fun at dinner."

"Thanks, Kelsey." Cheyenne gave her a tight hug, then left with Zach, leaving Bryce and Kelsey alone.

Bryce took a tentative step closer to Kelsey, running a hand through his hair. "Can we talk?"

"It won't matter, Bryce." She sank back into her chair, pulling the order form toward her and pretending to review it. But she couldn't see Bryce's chicken scratch—the same handwriting from the notes—through her tears.

He took a seat, too, choosing the chair beside hers instead of across the desk. "Did you get my notes?"

Kelsey didn't look up from the order form. "Yes. And I didn't think they were very funny."

"I wasn't trying to make you laugh." His tone was completely serious, with no hint of irony. "How can I make this up to you, Kelsey?"

"You said my sister's name," Kelsey choked out. She quickly brushed away a tear as it fell, hoping he hadn't noticed. But one quick glance told her he had.

"And I am so, so sorry for that." Bryce leaned forward, reaching for her hand, but she pulled away before he could grasp it. "I don't know what to say other than I obviously wasn't thinking."

She laughed, the sound hollow. "That's your excuse?"

"Not an excuse, but the truth." He scooted closer. "I was thinking about how grateful I was that I never asked Jadyn out in high school, because that would mean I wouldn't have a chance with you. I was thinking about how glad I was that you are here, and alive, and healthy. I was only thinking about *you*."

"You were really thinking that?" Her voice was a whisper, and she hated how hopeful it sounded.

Bryce's blue eyes were wide and shining with emotion. "Yes. Please, Kelsey. Give me a second chance."

She imagined agreeing to be Bryce's girlfriend, as he'd hinted in one of his notes. They'd send each other silly texts during down times at work and spend their non-working weekends at fan conventions and watching sci-fi shows. It was a beautiful picture—one she desperately wanted.

But she would always wonder if Bryce secretly wished he was with the other Wilkes sister.

"I can't." Kelsey brushed back more tears, focusing again on the order form. If her tears smeared it, they'd have to start all over, which would mean more time in this torturous office. "Please, let's hurry and finish this up so I can leave."

"It meant nothing, Kelsey," Bryce said, his voice thick with emotion.

His words pierced her heart. Did he mean the kiss, or saying Jadyn's name? "It meant something to me. I've spent a lifetime competing with Jadyn. I won't do it with you."

"There's no competition, because you've already won."

The words were perfect. A few days ago, before that fateful kiss, they would have made her heart leap with joy. But Kelsey shook her head, holding up the order form. "Okay, so Cheyenne decided on the calla lilies…"

Bryce stood abruptly, pushing his chair back abruptly. "I'm not giving up on us that easily."

"There's nothing to give up on!" she exclaimed. "You had a crush on Jadyn. You kissed me and said Jadyn. It's been her all along. I refuse to be my twin's stand-in."

"I had a crush on you first," Bryce said.

Kelsey looked up, startled. "What?"

Bryce nodded, his chest heaving. "When we were doing the biology project together. But you were always so quiet. Jadyn was always talking to me, though, and that's when my crush shifted to her."

She mulled over this information, letting it sink in. But it didn't change what had happened.

She turned back to the order form. "That doesn't change anything. I need someone who likes me for me, and not for who I look like."

"Your favorite part of wedding planning is the clients."

Kelsey looked up, startled. "What?"

He took a measured step toward her, moving around the desk. "You like organizing events, but what you really love is making couples happy. You'll bend over backwards to make sure their wedding day is perfect. I've seen it in the way you work with Cheyenne and Zach. You're an expert at helping brides and grooms compromise and have this magic ability to diffuse their stress."

She shook her head, struggling to keep up with this subject change. "What does this have to do with anything?"

He didn't bother to answer. Instead, his words kept coming, like a tsunami she was helpless to escape.

"You push the clicker on your pen an obnoxious number of times when you're concentrating. Your favorite music is country, but the modern stuff, not the old-timey twang. You like chocolate bars, but only if they don't have almonds in them. In fact, you don't like nuts in anything. Ice cream is your go-to dessert."

Kelsey leaned back in her chair as he reached for her hand. She let him pull her to her feet, holding her breath as she stared into his eyes.

"You'd rather sit at home and watch reality TV than go to a club or party. You're nerdy, but in a cute way. You love Doctor Who and Star Trek, but only the original series, not the new movies. You think Batman is the coolest of all the superheroes, even though it's totally Spider-Man. You twist your hair when you're nervous, but always notice after a moment and stop yourself."

"Why are you telling me things I already know?" Kelsey asked breathlessly. Her heart pounded in her chest, so loud she could hear it. Did Bryce hear it, too?

"Because I want you to understand that it's *you* I want to get to know better, Kelsey. It's you I'm crazy about."

She hadn't realized she'd tightened her grip on his hands until he gave them a reassuring squeeze in return. Bryce had noticed all those things about her? She'd had no idea he was watching her so closely.

"Jadyn was a crush I had a long time ago," Bryce said quietly. "But even if she were alive right now, standing next to you and begging me to go out with her, I'd pick you. Because you're the girl I want to date, Kelsey Wilkes. You're the girl I'm falling for."

Kelsey put a hand to her mouth, stifling a sob. "Since she died, everyone has either avoided me or wanted me to be her replacement."

"Not me," Bryce said, and there was a confidence in his tone she couldn't doubt. "I love you, Kelsey. I know it's too soon to say that, but I don't care because it's the truth. And I will do anything to make this up to you, if you'll just give me another chance."

Kelsey buried her face in Bryce's chest, her shoulders shaking with sobs. He loved her. Her! Not Jadyn. Because all of those things he'd mentioned? They were specific to her.

Bryce's arms came around her, one hand playing with her hair as he held her close.

"I'm falling in love with you, too," she whispered. "That's why it hurt so much when you said her name. It ripped me apart."

His lips brushed her hair, lingering against her forehead and sending a fire through her entire being. "I've been thinking about that all weekend. And I will prove to you, beyond a shadow of a doubt, that you're the twin for me."

Kelsey laughed, wrapping her arms around his waist and holding him close. "Are you sure I'm worth the effort?"

"Absolutely. How can I make it up to you? Name your price, and I'll pay it."

Kelsey peered up at him, making her tone teasing. "Do you finally concede that Batman is better than Spider-Man?"

Bryce didn't even grimace—just punched a fist into the air. "Long live Batman. He's the best."

Kelsey giggled, shaking her head. "You really do love me."

"I do."

He leaned forward, capturing her lips with his. Kelsey let herself sink into the kiss. Her hands threaded through his hair as his pressed against the small of her back, urging her closer. The stubble on his chin rubbed against her face in a way that made her skin tingle. One hand moved to cradle her face, angling it for a better kiss.

She'd never felt more cherished. More adored. More *her*.

And that's when Kelsey knew she'd spend the rest of her life kissing Bryce Michaels.

Chapter Sixteen

Kelsey looked around the Gardenia room at Magnolia Gardens with a satisfied smile. Cheyenne and Zach had just left amid a shower of rose petals to start their lives together as husband and wife. The day had gone perfectly, and the pure joy and happiness on Cheyenne and Zach's faces was worth the craziness of the last three months. This was the part of wedding planning Kelsey loved most—seeing all of her hard work and the bride's vision coming together in a perfect day that the couple would cherish for a lifetime.

Despite the bride and groom's departure, the Gardenia room was still half filled with people. Cheyenne had chosen an excellent DJ, and guests were still enjoying the dance floor.

Kelsey wandered over to the bar and reminded the bartender to close up shop at midnight. Loud music pounded through the room as guests laughed their way through the line dance that was playing at the moment.

She sank into a chair, her aching feet sighing happily in response. It had been a long, exhausting day, and she just wanted a few minutes to sit before the long, exhausting night of cleanup ahead of her. The white calla lily centerpiece obscured her vision of the dance floor, but she could see the caterers beginning to clear away the buffet line. Hopefully that would signal to the guests it was time to start winding things down.

Strong hands rested lightly on her shoulders. Kelsey looked up and Bryce's lips settled on hers. She grinned, wrapping her arms around his neck as he stood above her. His mouth was warm and tasted faintly of mint, and she relished in the taste of it.

The last couple of months as his girlfriend had been heaven. They'd spent every spare moment together. Long evenings spent kissing had set back their superhero rubric considerably, but they'd finally finished it last week and had watched their first superhero movie together— Batman, at Bryce's insistence. It had made Kelsey fall in love with him all over again.

"I was wondering when we'd get a chance to say hi," Kelsey said when Bryce finally let her up for air.

"Every time I've seen you today, you've been busy."

"Same," Kelsey agreed.

They'd had an absolute blast working on Cheyenne and Zach's wedding these past three months. Kelsey had been thrilled when another bride had chosen Magnolia Gardens just last week for a late winter wedding.

She knew it wouldn't be the same. The event coordinator would meet with Kelsey and her clients, while Bryce would be hard at work on putting together the marketing campaign Zach and Cheyenne had helped him with. But it would still be nice to work in the same building as him. To steal away for a quick kiss on occasion.

The music switched to a slow love ballad. Bryce took Kelsey's hand and tugged her to her feet, his eyes never leaving hers.

"Dance with me?" he asked.

"Okay," she agreed.

She was still mesmerized by his eyes. That dimple. Those lips. Bryce had confessed last month that he still had his trombone, and she'd convinced him to play her a song on it. He'd claimed to be rusty, but listening to him play had taken her back to watching him at football games all those years ago. She'd loved it just as much now as she had back then.

The dance floor had thinned. Across the floor, the bar was crowded as the thirsty dancers waited for a drink. Kelsey turned to Bryce, letting him pull her close as they swayed to the music. Cheyenne had chosen a dusky purple lighting scheme, and it bathed the Gardenia room in a romantic glow, casting shadows across the planes of Bryce's face. His warm hands rested at her waist while she threaded hers together at the back of his neck. She loved the way the soft curls at the nape of his neck sometimes brushed against her fingers as they danced.

"The ceremony and reception were beautiful," Bryce said. "The photographer let me peek at some of the shots."

"Any winners?" Kelsey asked.

Bryce nodded. "I can't wait to get started on the ad campaign."

"Brides are already flocking to this place. You've done such a great job with it."

"You were the one who did great." Bryce squeezed her waist, pulling her closer. "This place looks amazing."

"It was mostly Cheyenne's ideas. And your staff are the ones who implemented everything."

But Bryce was already shaking his head, that knee-melting dimple back in one cheek. "You're the one who brought Cheyenne's vision to life and helped translate it in a way that the staff could understand."

Kelsey ducked her head, feeling her cheeks burn while also loving the compliment. "Thank you."

"You're welcome."

"Cheyenne and Zach seemed happy with how today went, and the guests enjoyed themselves I think."

"Are still enjoying themselves." Bryce nodded to the bar with a smirk.

Kelsey laughed, nodding. "Yeah. And at the end of the day, that's all that really matters to me."

Bryce's eyes darkened. His fingers caressed her cheek, spreading fire through her limbs. "All that really matters to me is you."

The sincerity in his voice was unmistakable. Kelsey bit her lip, blinking back the sudden tears. "I love you so much," she whispered.

His hand moved from her waist to tangle in her hair. "I love you, too. We've had a good time the last few months, haven't we?"

"The very best. I haven't been this happy since Jadyn was alive." She bit her lip. "Maybe I wasn't even this happy then. You're everything to me now, Bryce."

"Kelsey." His voice was a breathy whisper as he crushed her to him.

The song had switched to a more upbeat one, and the dancers were back. But Bryce just held Kelsey to him, neither of them moving.

"I wasn't going to do this here. Not like this, anyway. But I can't wait any longer."

Kelsey pulled away, confused. "What are you talking about?"

"I'm talking about this." Bryce swallowed hard, then pulled a small velvet box from his pocket.

Kelsey gasped as he flipped it open. Nestled inside was a single diamond on a gold band. The lights of the dance floor caught on the diamond, sending a rainbow of light across Bryce's chest.

Her eyes flew up to his as one finger twisted around a strand of her hair. "Bryce..."

"I'm not very good at this kind of thing." Bryce cleared his throat, glancing at the ring. "I was going to take you back up to the Alpine Slide maybe, or plan some romantic dinner. But I can't wait any longer to ask you this question."

Kelsey couldn't stop staring at the ring. Her mouth felt like cotton, her throat blocked by the bowling ball she'd apparently swallowed. "And what question is that?" she managed to squeak out.

She hoped it was the question she'd been wanting him to ask for weeks. The one she'd told herself was much too soon to even think of.

"I love you, Kelsey," Bryce said simple. "I don't have any poetic words to say, or any speeches to make. But I've known I want to spend the rest of my life with you since our first kiss. And I know we haven't been dating very long, but I don't care. I know who you are, Kelsey Wilkes. And I'm not about to let you get away. Will you make me the happiest man on earth and be my wife?"

Kelsey pressed her hands to her stomach. "Are you sure?"

His eyes were steady and certain, and when his voice spoke it was strong. "I've never been more sure of something. You are my other half."

Kelsey put a hand to her mouth, the tears instantly pooling in her eyes. She'd thought that Jadyn was her other half. That she could never be whole without her.

But Bryce had proven that assumption wrong. He was her best friend. Her confidant.

Her soul mate.

"Yes." Kelsey laughed, nodding frantically. "Yes. I want to marry you."

Bryce grinned slipping the ring onto her finger—a perfect fit. Kelsey threw herself into his arms, kissing him until they were both breathless.

"I'm so grateful for grocery stores," Bryce said.

Kelsey laughed, nuzzling closer. "And my overpowering need for ice cream, no matter what time of day it is?"

Bryce laughed, kissing her. "That too."

"So am I." She leaned forward, capturing his lips in a slow kiss. "Because those two things brought me you. And I can't imagine spending the rest of my life with anyone else."

Epilogue

NINE MONTHS LATER

Jasmine spoke around the bobby pins in her mouth. "Just a second, I've almost got it..."

She stood on top of a Queen Anne chair, towering over Kelsey. Without her heels, Jasmine's flowing red Grecian-style dress pooled around her feet, looking like rose petals resting on the cream-colored chair cushion. She placed another bobby pin and Kelsey felt it prick her skull.

"Sorry," Jasmine said. "There. Tell me what you think."

Kelsey slowly turned and faced the full-length mirror in one corner of the bride's room at Magnolia Gardens. The veil was perfect, placed just at the crown of her head and trimmed in delicate lace. With trembling hands, she smoothed down the white satin of her dress.

"It's perfect," Kelsey said. "I feel like a princess. You did an amazing job on the dresses, Jas. We're the best dressed wedding party in the country."

"My dress would be nothing without the beautiful woman wearing it." Jasmine wrapped an arm around Kelsey's waist and their eyes met in the mirror. "You make an absolutely gorgeous bride."

Kelsey laughed, repositioning the jeweled belt at her waist. "I'm not used to being on this side of weddings."

"Well, it suits you." Jasmine grabbed a tissue from the vanity. "I swore I wasn't going to cry. I'm still furious at you for forcing a new neighbor on me."

"I know. I'll miss you, too." Kelsey hugged Jasmine close. Of course they'd still see each other, but it wouldn't be the same. "As soon as we finish remodeling the house, I'm inviting you over for an *Eye in the Sky* marathon. Promise."

Yesterday, Kelsey and Bryce had closed on a cute little house in the suburbs. It was small and needed a lot of work, but it had a fantastic den in the basement that they were excited to turn into a home theater. As soon as Kelsey and Bryce returned from their honeymoon to London, where they'd get to go on the Harry Potter Studios tour, they would start remodeling.

"If you'd told me a year ago that you'd be marrying Bryce today, I would have called you crazy," Jasmine said. "I thought for sure lying about Jadyn would end in disaster."

Kelsey shook her head, thinking of that first awkward meeting. She was so glad neither she nor Bryce had let it ruin their potential. "Bryce keeps assuring me that it's a great 'how we reconnected' story for the grandkids."

Jasmine snorted, then grabbed another tissue and dabbed at her eyes. "Yeah, it totally is. I'm so happy for you, Kels."

"Thank you." Kelsey squeezed Jasmine's hand, then glanced at the grandfather clock that sat against one wall. "Ten minutes. We need to make sure the last of the guests are taking their seats. The ushers should close the doors five minutes before the ceremony. Is the photographer in place? I want him at the front of the room near the minister so he can capture everything."

"Kelsey." Jasmine grabbed her hands, holding her gaze. "You're the bride today. The wedding planner has it all under control."

She was the bride. Kelsey took a slow, stuttering breath. This was her wedding. Her day.

The day she finally became Mrs. Bryce Michaels.

Her heart beat out a giddy rhythm and Kelsey put her hands to her flushed cheeks. She couldn't stop smiling. Her cheeks would probably ache by the end of the night, but she didn't care.

"Sorry," Kelsey said. "It's hard to switch from wedding planner mode to bride mode."

"I have faith that you can do it. Here." Jasmine grabbed her small red clutch off the vanity and opened it. She shook a mint from a container and held it out. "I might have borrowed your wedding day grab bag idea. Don't you always give your brides one of these before they walk down the aisle?"

Kelsey took the mint and placed it on her tongue. "Yes, I do. Maybe you should quit designing dresses and become a wedding planner."

Jasmine smirked. "Not a chance. I'll stick to fashion, thanks."

A soft knock sounded at the door. Kelsey turned, wondering if her mom had somehow sneaked back in. Liz, one of the wedding planners Kelsey had worked with at The Frosted Bride, had convinced her to take her seat a few minutes ago.

But it was Liz, not Kelsey's mom, who stood in the doorway. She offered a warm smile and simply said, "It's time."

Kelsey pressed her trembling hands against her stomach. "I'm ready."

She met her father outside the double French doors leading into the Gardenia room and gave him a tight hug. His eyes glistened with tears, and Kelsey knew there were sad ones mingled with the happy. It was impossible not to miss Jadyn on a day like this.

Kelsey leaned forward, giving her dad a tight hug.

"You'll mess up your hair," he muttered, but didn't loosen his hold.

"I don't care," Kelsey said. "I love you, Dad."

"I love you too, sweetheart. And we love Bryce, too."

Kelsey grinned, nodding to Liz. The wedding planner sprung into action, motioning for the ushers to open the doors. Jasmine gave Kelsey one last grin, then straightened her shoulders and headed down the aisle.

"Are you nervous?" Dad asked, patting Kelsey's hand.

"No," she answered honestly. "I'm just happy."

The wedding march began. Now the Pop Rocks weren't just jumping in her stomach—they were giving off more of a Mentos-and-Coke feeling.

"Let's do this," she whispered.

Kelsey took her first step down the white aisle strewn with wild flowers. Guests stood to either side of her, their smiles wide and encouraging. She saw her mother in the front row, dabbing at her eyes with a tissue.

But it was Bryce who captured and held Kelsey's attention. He stood at the end of the aisle underneath a canopy of red balloons, in a black tuxedo and red vest and tie. Her heart soared at the sight of him, and she had to consciously will herself not to sprint down the aisle.

His eyes glistened as he watched her, grinning until his dimple made its appearance. Love shone from his expression, reaching down the aisle and wrapping itself around her heart. He looked as inviting as a cold Dr. Pepper on a hot day. Bryce was a chocolate bar and double chocolate fudge brownie ice cream all rolled into Batman jammies and reality TV.

Kelsey's heart nearly exploded with happiness. There was sadness, too—just a tinge—that Jadyn wasn't standing at the front as her maid of honor. But Kelsey couldn't help thinking that this was how it was supposed to have happened all along.

Maybe, just maybe, Jadyn had been the one to orchestrate her meeting with Bryce at the grocery store exactly one year ago. And as Bryce stood beneath the archway of red balloons, Kelsey knew she had her sister's blessing.

At the front of the aisle, Kelsey's dad kissed her cheek, then placed her hand in Bryce's. Fire ignited at his touch, flowing hot and quick through her veins. Even after a year, he still had that effect on her. She wanted to caress that dimple with her fingertips. Lose herself in his arms. But there would be time enough for that later. Right now, it was time to become his wife.

The minister invited the crowd to sit, and the ceremony began. Kelsey barely heard the ceremony as she and Bryce had a silent conversation that needed no words. They recited traditional vows, their eyes never leaving each other's.

"I now pronounce you husband and wife," the minister said. "You may now kiss the bride."

Bryce didn't need any further encouragement. She gasped as he wrapped an arm tightly around her waist, pulling her toward him. Her hands threaded through his hair and the watching crowd disappeared in the face of the passion seething just beneath the surface.

"I love you, Mrs. Michaels," Bryce whispered, caressing the red balloon tattoo behind her ear.

She looked at the ceiling, sighing happily. "You have no idea how long I've waited to hear that."

The crowd cheered, and Kelsey laughed as Bryce took her hand and led her back down the aisle.

"This is it," Bryce said, pausing just before the double doors.

Kelsey raised one eyebrow. "What?"

"The start of the rest our lives. Are you ready for it?"

Kelsey squeezed Bryce's hand, then pushed open the doors. "Absolutely."

About the Author

LINDZEE ARMSTRONG is the *USA Today* bestselling author of more than twenty romances. She met her true love while at college, where she graduated with a bachelor's in history education. They are now happily married and raising twin boys in the Rocky Mountains. Like any true romantic, Lindzee loves chick flicks, ice cream, and chocolate. She believes in sigh-worthy kisses and happily ever afters, and loves expressing that through her writing.

To find out about future releases, you can join Lindzee's reader's club. You can also find her on her website, www.LindzeeArmstrong.com.

If you enjoyed this book, please take a few minutes and leave a review. This is the best way you can say thank you to an author! It really helps other readers discover books they might enjoy. Thank you!

Made in the USA
Columbia, SC
18 October 2024

44276323R00081